# THERAPY
# FOR
# GHOSTS

*A Novel*

ERIC PRASCHAN

To Sharmini,
  Thanks for your support!
  I hope you enjoy the book.
        All the best,
        Eric Prasch

ISBN-13: 978-0988174702
ISBN-10: 0988174707
LCCN: 2012914357

Visit www.amazon.com to order additional copies.

For my wife, Stephanie.
My voice of reason, my sunshine, my marvelous treasure.
Thank you for always believing.

# *Acknowledgements*

To Duane and Judy Praschan, Dad and Mom, for lifelong support, love, and wisdom. To Uncle Jim and Aunt Mary Lou Harman for sharing the hope of eagles. To the rest of my family and friends.

To Nathan Nelson, Sandy Vekasy, and Marilyn Quigley for affirming my love of literature. To Craig Froman for encouraging me to find my writer's voice. To Lois Olena for challenging me to forgo the glamor and write from the gut.

To Amanda Capps, my editor, for believing in the story and injecting genius into it as needed. To Ray Blackston for a timely critique and for proving it's possible to defy conventionality and pursue "this writing thing."

You're all a part of this long-awaited dream becoming reality.

# THERAPY
# FOR
# GHOSTS

# *Chapter One*

*Mama, I've been remembering you, and that scares me to death. These static days and sleepless nights have brought her back to me, the young girl covering her ears and cowering beneath her bed in terror. Our unspoken pact to forget is at risk. I wish you were here to guide me through the darkness, to remind me how to rid ourselves of what she has seen and what she knows, yet I am glad you are gone, because you will not have to face her again. She is coming for me, and I have run out of places to hide.*

I stir awake, feeling sweat burning my body. My foggy eyes stare at the ceiling, waiting for the shadows amid the candlelight to shift. All stays still in the room, reminding me that there is no one else with whom to share the nightmares. I peel back the freshly ironed bed sheets and slide my feet into cushioning slippers. After slipping on my robe, I tiptoe to the bedroom door, undo the two deadbolt locks, and step into the drafty hallway, all the while seeking to purge the vivid mental image of the little girl hiding beneath her bed and covering her ears in dread.

In the darkness of the interior, the house features are not clearly visible, but I have walked these halls enough at night to know them blindly. The middle section of varnished wood down each hall has a faint, grooved indention from my countless footsteps traversing back and forth during post-nightmare purging sessions. A gaping space sits at the center of the house's five levels, forming an atrium around which the rectangular levels of each hallway are built. At the four corners of each level is a wooden staircase. Every night I walk up and down the levels, glancing through the open doorways of the rooms to see the shadow-pressed presence of candlelight burning with tiny vigor only inches away from closed window curtains.

When I return to my starting point, if the mental image still has not vanished—like tonight—I make my way to the cherry wood door which stands alone on the far wall of the third level.

Upon prying open the only door besides my own which remains closed at night, I enter an empty fifteen-foot by fifteen-foot room. Tonight the windowless, candle-less space appears darker than usual, forcing my eyes to squint in an effort to detect the color consuming the room. The walls, ceiling, and floor are a distinct, rich red, a shade which has only seemed to darken since the day I painted it liberally with a brush that was just one inch wide. For the life of me, however, I still cannot remember why I painted the room red.

While moving to the center of the room, I find the only occupant lying in one of her sleeping spots. Kneeling down, I pick up the headless Raggedy Ann doll and hold her reverently. The image of the girl hiding beneath the bed in terror creeps into my mind, but I dismiss it abruptly, choosing instead to clutch the doll tightly to my chest. Then I pry her away from me and gently lower her back onto the floor. I stretch out, lie beside her, and press my face against the cold, spotless hardwood. Tears fall from my eyes to puddle on the comfortless floor. The memory flash bursts like a reckless spark, igniting my kindled thoughts with the urge to remember.

I open my eyes and the foggy features of my office come into focus. I see blonde-haired Samantha Jackson standing stiffly in the doorway with mascara smudges gleaming beneath her eyes. "What if he doesn't think I'm worth the effort it will take to change his behavior?"

I smile knowingly. "Samantha, if you won't breach this subject with him, then you're going to keep pacifying the very thing that damages you. I wouldn't be a good friend if I were any less honest."

She gathers herself with a reassuring breath. "Thanks, Cindy. Talking with you helps give me the courage I'll need to face him. Sometimes it feels like I'm still coming to you for therapy instead of just being a friend catching up. Well, I've got to get home and cook dinner. Hope he comes home sober tonight." She expels a weighty sigh and then smiles grimly. "See you soon, Cindy."

"See you, Samantha."

After she disappears down the hallway, I move to the door and close it quietly. Then I slump down in the office chair, hoping the heaviness in my limbs will subside. Three stacks of paper sit in evenly distributed piles on the far right corner of the finely polished cherry wood desk. A "Time" magazine lies just below the paper piles, marked with today's date, April 1, 1995. An ornate desk lamp rests beside a brass square holder filled with uniform pens. A single picture surrounded by a simple glass frame occupies the space on the far left corner of the desk, a wrinkled three by five photo of Mama and me in my pink walled bedroom when I was thirteen years old. I find myself staring at the picture far longer than I intended, beginning to travel back in memory, dazed in emotional fog.

Brushing off the sensation, I slip on my coat and grab my purse on the way out of the room, seeing Samantha's jacket—which she always used to leave behind in my house when she was a patient ten years ago—still draped around the coat stand. As I lock the office door, an odd tingling pricks my thigh and calf muscles. My vision becomes blurry, almost double. I stagger to the outer door, open it, and scarcely step outside before my fingers fumble and release the keys. The sound of clinking metal rattles from the concrete below. I attempt to reach down and retrieve the keys, but my arm feels as if it is struggling against a wave of water. A bizarre, unbalanced sensation swarms over my joints. Each muscle feels plunged into molasses, wobbling in painful slow motion, as if weighed down by lead. I attempt to scream for help, but my mouth remains closed and unresponsive. My eyes grow wide with alarm. Both weightless and immensely heavy, my body teeters, my knees buckle, and I ungracefully careen backward onto the concrete sidewalk. I lie motionless, sensing terror quicken my heartbeat and restrict my breathing.

*Breathe, Cindy, keep breathing. You're having a panic attack, nothing more. Focus on breathing.*

A full minute passes and my limbs lay limp without response.

*Just breathe, keep breathing.*

Another minute passes. Still nothing.

*Someone, please come. Keep breathing, Cindy. Someone has to come.*

My consciousness ebbs and I surrender to the mental void.

The memory flash continues propelling me forward, pricking my thoughts with the pull of remembrance.

My eyelids quiver, trying to open themselves. The throbbing in my backside informs me I am lying on a bed of some kind. The joints in my arms and legs pulse with dulling pain. A disturbing calm blankets each nerve. The desire to rest and remain unmoving beckons strongly, but I do not want to sleep for fear I may not awaken again.

"While I was driving home, I realized I had forgotten my jacket, so I turned around to go back to her office." Samantha's excitable voice echoes throughout the room. "When I got there, she was on the ground, not moving or speaking."

"I'm just glad you found her," Jody Simon's voice replies with an even higher pitch. I picture Jody's sparkling blue eyes and fiery red hair, her pretty face frazzled with concern.

Authoritative footsteps enter the room, precise in their cadence and deliberate in their direction.

"Ms. James, can you hear me?" A man's deep, commanding voice bludgeons my ears. "If you can hear me, open your eyes."

My brain gives the signal, but my eyelids are defiant.

*Concentrate, Cindy. The sooner you open your eyes, the sooner you can leave.*

I open my eyelids shakily, overwhelmed by the blinding fluorescent light above. My eyes rove in his direction and detect a tall, bearded black man in an angel-white jacket.

"My name is Dr. Shipper. I'm the neurologist on duty in the hospital right now. Can you follow my finger?"

His slender finger appears in front of my face and he waves it from side to side while my eyes try to track it.

"Good, Ms. James. Can you speak to me?"

My eyes stare at him, desperate to communicate something, anything.

He smiles knowingly. "That's all right. We'll get there. The MRI, the CT scan, the spinal tap, and the blood work came back negative. The only logical conclusion we can reach is that you experienced some type of stress disorder reaction. It appears that either the unprocessed accumulation of stress or some unresolved trauma in your mind has caused your body to mimic symptoms of health conditions you do not have. The body is reacting in a physical manner to something psychological. I want you to see a cognitive behavioral therapist."

The ladies stand speechless. My eyes search his helplessly.

Jody smirks. "She *is* a cognitive behavioral therapist."

He smiles supremely, eyeing me with a knowing gleam. "Then I suppose it will be quite an interesting experience for you.

I want you to see a friend of mine, Tony Prost. He's new in town. I'll schedule an appointment for you and write down his address and phone number on your discharge papers. I don't want you working for at least a week. Your body should regain strength soon. Once you're able to speak and walk, you are free to go. I'll be back to check on you in a little while."

Without another word, he nods and makes his way out of the room, leaving us bewildered.

The mental flash returns me to the red room floor. I close my eyes and continue grappling with images of the young girl hiding beneath her bed and covering her ears to block out the horrid sounds coming from somewhere else in her house. I reach out and pull Raggedy Ann tightly to myself. I don't have the heart to tell her that the real agony is about to begin. Something is stirring deep within my memory, and I don't know how to keep it a secret from myself any longer; this time, it will consume me.

# Chapter Two

Today is my third day on house arrest within these embittered walls. I have tasked myself with dusting and scrubbing each room until it is spotless. Thirty-one rooms in three days. Mama would be proud.

As I recline on the armchair in the library on the first level, I skim through *Wuthering Heights*, observing pen-marked notations in the margins that I made during previous readings. My calloused fingers turn the pages, aching with overuse. My knees groan from bending down and wiping baseboards clean. Every muscle throbs and my head is spinning from inhaling excess cleaning sprays.

I close the book, lay it to rest on the end table beside me, and stare out the window, which is finely dressed with lavender satin curtains, curtains that are most often closed. The afternoon sunlight has been peeking into the room for the past several hours, warming the wooden floor, which in turn warms my bare, blistered feet. Fatigue flirts with me for a few more minutes until I am fully seduced. My eyelids grow weighty, unable to suspend the hope that today will bring anything other than enduring silence. As I drift into dreams, I imagine myself floating around these levels like a disenchanted ghost, dreading this haunting dwelling place, yet even more terrified by my own ghastly existence.

*Mama, I've been wandering through this house again, trying to find some measure of peace. There is no heart left in this multi-level tomb. I don't have the strength to fill these rooms with all that a house needs to become a home. I am no more woman than half of you, and each day you remain gone reminds me of my un-wholeness.*

*As I wander these halls, I feel the loneliness hanging like a suffocating fog. The open cavity between the levels brings me closer to stepping into the void. If only I might fall into it and descend from my disorder, releasing the hope that I can change. Surely you also wanted to jump and end it all at some point.*

*This house feels as hollow as my heart, and the red room, where I remember the best and the worst of you, still paints each memory dark.*

*This health episode in my body is causing the awakening of something buried long ago in my nightmares, something I'm not sure I'm ready to revisit. I need to know you're still here, wanting what is best for me. I need you now, more than I have ever needed you since the day I lost you.*

Suddenly, I find myself staring at my own reflection in a tall, oval mirror. At first, my features exhibit a deathly pallor which steals my breath away. The rich blood of youth has drained from my face. Coal black hairs around my scalp have frosted with wintry decay. My breathing is labored, coming forth in constricted, apnea-like gasps. In every limb, I see frail bones and sagging muscles struggling to support a weakened woman.

Then, the chalky hue in my skin warms to a peach color. Health blossoms in my cheeks, my lips redden with vigor, and my figure, though clad in crude cleaning clothes, finds a stance of power as my hands rest firmly on my hips. A smile akin to something almost confident graces my mouth. A gust of life sweeps into my lungs. I see Cindy as I do not know her, and my previously heavy eyelids now blink away endearing tears rather than exhausting slumber.

Yet I find myself missing her already because I am sure I will never know this woman before me. I sense I will be gone in less than one of these idealistic breaths, reduced to the shackling sentence of scrubbing and dusting these thirty-one rooms, sweeping and mopping these endless hallways, and spot polishing the red room inch by inch until I am reduced to the figureless form of a ghost forever haunted by these halls.

Without more than another fleeting moment to view myself with this longing image of empowerment, I watch as the reflection changes once again. Drops of blood trickle down from my nose, the fair skin on my cheeks swells with deep purple bruising, and a headless Raggedy Ann doll appears in my clutching hands. I watch this woman viewing me with sadness in her eyes. I long to comfort her and give her hope that her future will be better than her present. I want her to understand that someday she will escape. But I cannot say these things to her with certainty, so I stare at her in silence and we watch each other's tears running down our faces. I cannot bear to see her anymore, so I say good-bye and close my eyes.

I awaken suddenly, my neck and arms twitching erratically. I stare at the ceiling and breathe deeply, trying to calm my thoughts while feeling the rush of my panicked breath. My skin is slick with sweat.

Shivering, I fetch my robe and wander out into the hallway. With a luring lean against the banister, I overlook the void between the levels. The space appears endless in the darkness. I perceive its pull. I long to climb this banister and release myself into nothing.

*Don't judge me, Mama. The world to me is empty. I see no outcome other than the inevitable descent.*

I continue looking out across the dark expanse, allowing the brooding to deepen within me. Falling would bring me escape, the freedom I have craved all these years. Surely no one will miss an obscure woman whose carefully marked life lines were too rigid to permit a dish washing, baby making, apron wearing convention to fit around her figure. Days would pass before I was discovered, and even then, Samantha and Jody would be the only funeral attendees.

I can picture them with their compact kits held tightly in their flawlessly manicured hands, ready to refresh their makeup with each perfunctory tear that falls. There are no flowers, there is no casket, there is not even a formal funeral service. Instead, they stand in the red room, peering closely into their compact kit mirrors because the boarded up window disallows natural light to give them a better view of themselves. Lying in the middle of the floor is my ghostly body, headless, but not grotesquely headless—just an empty space where my head should be, as if having been erased by the backspace key on my work computer. Clutched in my dead arms is Raggedy Ann, her head sewn on and her eyes looking up blankly, with her yarn smile naively fixed. Samantha and Jody shed two more tears a piece in tandem before closing their compact kits and exiting the makeshift funeral home, their high heels tapping on the wooden floor click—click—click.

Left alone with my lifeless body and my stilled thoughts, I release one hand from Raggedy Ann's torso and use it to cover her eyes. There we remain, our bodies pinned against each other, one girl headless and the other girl sightless, both of us hoping we can force ourselves to forget what happened.

I continue gazing into the gaping void, sensing it tugging at me, drawing me closer to its alluring abyss.

*I struggle with who I am to be as a woman, Mama. I feel the pull of expected domesticity: 1) Find a suitable soul mate—just pick him out of the crowd like choosing the perfect White Elephant gift at a Christmas party; 2) Marry that miracle man and discover the fulfillment that I am apparently devoid of without him; 3) Football snap babies out of my uterus to become playthings for the miracle man; and, finally, 4) Grow weak, wrinkled, and denture-destined while wearing away the skin on my hands and knees scrubbing to keep clean the disorder that has overtaken my life.*

*Sorry, Mama, but it's not for me. Freedom is my only security, and the only freedom I can have is in a world where I control the outcomes. Anything else will only expose me to pain. I must make my own way, even though it is not a way you would have taken. I cannot afford to take your path; it will surely destroy me.*

After pulling my leaning head away from looming over the banister, I release my grip on the railing, head back into my room, double lock the door, and spend a moment retrieving an object from beneath the bed. Climbing into bed, I sling the covers on top of me and quietly curl up, grasping headless Raggedy Ann to my chest. We stay together through the restless night until the dawn arrives, trying in vain to forget that tomorrow is going to change everything.

# *Chapter Three*

As I drive across town, I survey the conventional quality of Sleepy Oak, Missouri. The picket fences wearing white to fulfill picturesque dreams. The ranch style homes with porch swings, groomed shrubs, and lush flower beds planted from pages of "Better Homes and Gardens." Children's bicycles lying collapsed in front yards as if piled against makeshift bike racks of grass. Newborns and toddlers being chauffeured around in four-wheel drive strollers by figure form moms fashioning slimming jeans and tan-accenting sunglasses. Sleek minivans sitting parked in Nerf football and Barbie doll-filled driveways. I watch this town click in my brain like a snapshot, the same picture taken over twenty years ago that Mama must have witnessed when we first rolled by in the rusty pickup truck while I was asleep.

I swerve my blue Ford Taurus into a narrow parking lot.

*Deep breaths, Cindy, you can do this. Only an hour of less than straightforward answers and then you can accept the business card he will certainly offer. Of course, you will conveniently forget to call and schedule a follow-up appointment. This is the sacrifice required in order to return to work. Normalcy depends on this visit, so give this guy an hour of little to work with and then you can get back to your life.*

I exit the car with my purse and jacket in hand. My eyes veer over to the other car two spaces away, a white, dirt covered Pontiac Grand Am, complete with all the wear marks you would expect from poor upkeep and what must certainly be 200,000 miles plus of aimless travel. My feet suddenly feel frozen to the pavement as I glance at the modest brick establishment and the white-lettered sign gleaming with fresh paint: *Tony Prost Cognitive Behavioral Therapy*.

I breathe deeply and head to the front door. Once inside, I cross a short hallway to find a quaint reception area consisting of two waiting chairs and a put-it-together-yourself particle board table that must have been a discount purchase from Walmart. The table holds a smattering of CBT pamphlets and pop culture magazines, as well as a glass candy bowl which calls out to me with its tempting content of Hershey's Kisses.

A white door stands on either side of the reception area. The door on the left has a dull silver placard labeled *Conference Room*, while the door on the right is labeled *Tony Prost*. I motion to knock on the right door, but then withdraw my hand. I quickly turn and find my hand making a desperate dash for the candy bowl. No sooner have my greedy fingers splashed into the bowl to secure a Hershey's Kiss than the office door swings open.

"I see you found the truth serum," an offbeat, strong voice echoes in my ears.

I yank my hand out of the bowl, my cheeks turning red, and land my embarrassed gaze on a medium-tall, fairly tanned man.

"I was—just checking something," I stammer.

I give him the once over, noticing his high cheekbones, somewhat narrow nose, and olive eyes. He appears to be in his mid-thirties, with a few strands of gray spotting his otherwise light brown hair. Clad in a flannel red shirt and faded blue jeans beginning to fray at the inseams, he appears far too casual and not quite handsome enough to gawk at or merit categorical cuteness.

"Don't worry," he says with a wry smile. "Most people who visit here also end up needing to check something in that bowl. Why don't you come on in?"

He leads the way into his office, while I follow him timidly. He closes the door as I glance around to take in the scene. Weak coffee colored carpet—a murky brown tint already splotched with two beverage stains—supports the office furniture. A black wooden desk sits in the left corner, swamped with unorganized paperwork. Two dark green couches are set on opposite walls, surrounding an oval coffee table. As predicted, another comforting candy bowl waits atop the coffee table. My eyes scan the walls, discovering a framed photo of him and two other men posing in front of the St. Louis Arch, and another framed photo of the three amigos at a St. Louis Cardinals game. I sense his eyes searching my scrutinizing gaze.

"I'm Tony Prost, by the way, but I'm sure you already know that."

My eyes reluctantly agree to meet his. "I'm Cindy James, CBT," I offer, shaking his hand politely and sensing a strange acceptance coming from the laid back yet firm grip of his hand.

"Nice to meet you," he continues dutifully. "Why don't we get started?" Then he points to the couches. "Pick your poison and I'll take the other one."

I watch him, a bit taken aback, as he saunters over to the desk and rifles through the paperwork pile haphazardly. After observing him unearth a slew of teeth-marked pens, as well as a second layer of mish-mashed forms hiding beneath the initial surface layer of papers, I wonder if I will be the one who actually needs therapy between the two of us.

*Just an hour, Cindy, just an hour.*

I discreetly move to sit on the couch farthest from his desk, setting down my coat and purse and waiting for him to conclude his desk-top rummage sale.

"Where's that pen?" he asks aloud, hoping someone in the room more sensible and organized will know the answer. "Sorry," he mutters over his shoulder. "I have a favorite pen that I use and— here it is."

He arises from the rubble presenting a half-gnawed blue Bic pen, the seventy-nine-cent variety he must have found and tossed into his shopping cart en route to the put-it-together-yourself reception table at Walmart. He brings the pen and a pad of ink-scribbled paper over to the opposing green couch and plops down unprofessionally. I stare at him, trying to decide if I want to be amused or disgusted.

"Before we start, I need to know something," he states confidently, as if preparing to launch into a well-rehearsed introduction leading to some type of evidence that he is indeed a competent therapist and not an escaped patient from the psych ward across town.

"What's that?" I offer, maintaining a reserved tone.

"Do you still want a piece of chocolate? Because I certainly do."

He waits for the startled reaction to crisscross my face and then he reaches over to the coffee table and picks out a Hershey's Kiss for me and one for himself. With cavalier nonchalance, he tosses the chocolate piece to me. I catch the prize awkwardly and fumble it in my hands as redness colors my face. As I glance down at the tasty nemesis, I feel his eyes searching me.

I hear him peeling the wrapper from his piece and I sense the freedom to do the same. Without looking up at him, I undo the wrapper and pop the treasure into my mouth. My taste buds express their gratitude as the rich sweetness finds itself quickly chewed and swallowed. For a moment, the dark trauma and troubles lurking just below the surface of my thoughts vanish. The chocolate—like so many other foods secretly consumed for comfort—works its magic, allowing me to suppress the rising memories and escape their grasp, if only for a moment. I fully swallow before looking up at him.

"Like I said, it's truth serum. Chocolate is my confession drug of choice," he says, grinning.

My eyes cover his features once more, surprised by their plainness and the latitude they afford him at the expense of my having believed him to be unassuming and clueless.

"Are you always this casual in your sessions?" I hear myself blurt out.

"Not always, although I try to be," he responds, straight-faced.

"Okay—"

"Does it bother you?" he asks, probing my eyes.

*Relax, Cindy, stay calm.*

"I'm just not used to it, that's all. I was trained to be a bit more, well, a bit more formal."

He smiles. "I was too, but it never took. Another chocolate?"

"No," I reply, raising my palms toward him. "One is good enough—or bad enough." I smile sheepishly, both flustered and irritated.

He nods. "Understood. So, do you have the forms I sent you?"

"Yes," I reply, unzipping my purse, retrieving the carefully creased paperwork, and extending it across the coffee table and into his hand. Once he receives the paperwork, I quickly zip my purse and fold my sweating hands properly on my lap.

He leans back on the couch, leafing through the forms and double checking for my consent signatures. He seems to mumble something to himself and then he looks up at me. "So you don't want this session to be audio recorded?"

"No," I answer quickly.

"Not a problem. Although perhaps after another chocolate you'll feel differently." Again, he waits for shock to register on my face. "Just kidding," he adds dryly. "Sorry, you'll have to excuse my methodology at times."

"How long have you been a therapist?"

"Ten years," he answers, unflappable.

"And where did you study?"

"B.A. in psychology from the University of Missouri Saint Louis. Master of Social Work from the University of Tennessee. I never hang my diplomas on the wall because it feels pretentious to me. Or maybe it's because I always forget to hang them. I can never remember which is the real reason."

"Oh," I say softly.

"Again, I apologize if my way of conducting sessions is unorthodox." Then, without missing a beat, he smiles and says, "So, let's begin, unless you have any other questions about my credibility?"

*Just an hour, Cindy, just an hour. Circumvent this buffoon with some vague answers and you'll be out of here in no time.*

"No further questions," I respond, faux-submissively.

With a smile and nod of affirmation, he puts his pen up to his mouth and chews on the end of it while glancing down once more at my paperwork in his hands. Then he looks up and arrests my attention with his gaze.

"I know you know how these sessions are supposed to go. The first session is a get-to-know each other time. Not much deep digging. Obviously, nothing discussed leaves this room. You're going to feel free to be honest with me only if you believe that I'm not here as a judge demanding behavioral modifications for thought processes deemed wrong. There is no right and wrong in this room; it is only about dealing with perceptions that may be impeding you from healthy stress management. I'm not in the business of trying to correct you. I'm simply a sounding board who is walking with you, not an authoritarian who is telling you where to walk. Is this acceptable to you?"

I fidget with my fingers, absorbing his words and the earnest expression on his face. "I understand how it works. We can cut to the chase. I don't want to take up too much of your time."

"Actually, I thought you might want to know a bit about me. I've had a head start on the chocolate today, so I'll spill first," he replies, his eyes begging me to smile.

I half-smile, not willing to humor him completely.

"Okay," I say, feeling a bit relieved.

"I've been a Missourian most of my life, born and raised in a small suburb outside of St. Louis. Never traveled into the city except for the zoo, the Arch, and the Cardinals. I've been a licensed therapist for ten years, as I already mentioned. My father was a therapist and he started me down this path. No wife, no kids. The only time I've lived outside of Missouri is when I completed my MSW at the University of Tennessee. I wanted to see the South without going as far as Alabama or Georgia. Sweet tea is king in the South, you know? Had to try it for myself, so I figured I would pick up a master's degree while hanging out there. I moved here to start my own practice after having worked in other people's businesses for a few years. Too tired of political haranguing with senior staff and enforcing policy for upstart youngsters who are proof positive that they think they know better. I'm 36, a fan of small, quaint Americana like this unassuming town of Sleepy Oak here. That about covers it. Any questions?"

I wish I had another Hershey's Kiss to distract me. I wait for him to continue speaking, scratching my fingernails together and casting my gaze around the room, trying to act absent-minded. He answers me with contented silence, those unnerving eyes doing their best to form-fit my puzzle pieces together.

"That's interesting," I say, uninterested. "When did you move in here?"

"Four weeks ago. The paint's barely dried on this place. Got the building in a shrewd deal with a low-life Missouri mob member."

I shoot him a wary glance and his amused eyes express how easy of a target I am. Nevertheless, I appease him with a smile, counting minute number fifteen out of sixty being checked off of the list in my head. *Good work, Cindy. Let him wallow in the satisfaction of his own self-indulgent humor.*

"There's a smile," he says, victoriously. "Now, let's get down to the good stuff. Of course, John Shipper referred you to me. He told me about your health episode last week. That's some scary crap. Pardon my crude vernacular. I couldn't think of another word to describe it, other than scary." His eyes survey mine, finding no reciprocal jovial quality in them. Surprisingly, he leaves the moment alone, not accentuating the tension with another smart remark. "So why don't you tell me about yourself? The therapist in me wants to know everything from the beginning. The man in me wants to know far less."

My eyes cannot contain their shock. "Excuse me?" I ask sharply.

"Just seeing if you're still listening. Your focus keeps drifting elsewhere, as if intent to make me follow a deliberate diversion. Surely, as a therapist yourself, you know how disconcerting that can be."

"I must say, Mr. Prost, this is incredibly awkward behavior on your part. Your manner of speaking to a patient is rude and uncouth." I sense the color in my face rising in redness.

"So, you *have* been paying attention. Please, feel free to begin at any time. Tell me how your thought process about yourself is not important enough to give us anything to talk about." His eyes sparkle with recognition.

"That's an unfair assumption, Mr. Prost. As therapists, we are to avoid such categorical assertions." My eyes glower with frustration.

"Fair enough," he announces, leaning forward to toss the chewed pen and pad of paper onto the coffee table. "It's been a long time since I've counseled another therapist, and it seems like an equally long time since you've allowed someone to counsel you. Seeing that this is relatively uncharted territory for both of us, I'll let you take the lead. Divulge only what you desire for me to know, and I will do my best not to antagonize you for information you wish to leave unknown."

I stare at him with scathing intensity for a moment. Then I allow our eyes to reach a truce. *Only forty minutes left, Cindy. You're a third of the way home.*

"Very well. My name is Cindy James. I've been a CBT for a little less than ten years. B.A. in psychology from the University of

Missouri Kansas City. Master of Social Work from the University of Missouri Kansas City. I hang my diplomas on my office wall so no one has to guess whether I'm qualified to counsel them. I've lived here in Sleepy Oak for as long as I can remember. My significant stressors of the past twenty-two years are—in chronological order—as follows: puberty; college; a traumatic, uneven haircut I received on my twenty-first birthday; the time spent waiting for the re-growth of the uneven haircut; graduate school; testing for state licensure; earning national certification; starting my own practice as a therapist; cleaning the house; falling into temporary paralysis last week; and seeing you today. That about covers it. Any questions?"

My steely stare is unflinching. His mouth does not forfeit a smile, but his eyes dance. "Very good, Ms. James. Now we are getting somewhere."

I bite my lower lip and glance down dramatically at my watch. "I'm sorry, but I just realized I have to go. It's work related." I stand up hastily.

He smiles. "Of course. You've been put on house arrest from work this week, so naturally you have to return to work. I completely understand."

I laugh nervously. "It's not what it seems. I need to prepare for returning to work, and I have an appointment I must keep. I'll still pay you for the full hour."

He waves his hand. "Not necessary. Surely a session between the only two CBTs in this small town can be done free of charge. We're on the same side anyway, right?"

"Apparently so. Thank you." I hear my voice coming out weakly.

"Don't mention it," he says, casually rising to his feet.

I grab my purse and coat. "I guess I'll see you around town or something, since you seem to be working here now." I move quickly to the door.

"Well, from the way I see it, you still owe me half an hour," he states firmly.

I stop and stare at him. "What?"

"You're running out early on our session, so you'll need to come back to finish the last half hour. Standard procedure with me. How is Tuesday at 6 p.m.?"

"Um—" I struggle, opening the door and inching out into the hallway. "That works, I guess."

"Great, I'll see you then. A half hour more and you won't have to see me ever again, I promise. Just think of it as a ransom payment to purchase your freedom."

I laugh awkwardly and glance back to see strange understanding in his eyes, the same unabated acceptance I found in his handshake when I first entered the room. "Sure, that's one way to look at it," I offer.

"Do you want a chocolate for the road?" he asks, tilting his head toward the bewitching bowl on the coffee table.

"No. Thank you. I have to go."

With a swift motion, I close his office door behind me. After a quick, steadying breath, I reach for the candy bowl on the particle board reception table and secure a Hershey's Kiss. Then I walk speedily across the hallway, finding the outer door within moments. Careful not to glance back to see if he has opened his office door and peered around the corner to watch me depart, I push open the door and hustle out to my waiting car, gripping the chocolate between my fingers.

# *Chapter Four*

"So, what was he like?" Jody asks, sitting across from me at the white and black checker topped table, finally crossing into territory I know both she and Samantha have been itching to visit since we arrived at the diner ten minutes ago.

The atmosphere buzzes with chattering voices and Elvis singing about his blue suede shoes. The classic 1950s car pictures on the walls and mini-juke boxes begging for quarters at the table ends remind me of what must have been a simpler time, something that seems foreign indeed.

"Cindy, you still with us?" Jody's voice penetrates my ears. I realize my eyes have been roaming around the room as much as my thoughts have been disjointed.

"Sorry, just zoned out for a moment," I reply, trying to conceal an embarrassed smile.

"Thinking about the new therapist?" Samantha asks from beside me, her face glowing.

"That's ridiculous," I counter sharply.

"How was he? We need details," Jody urges.

I roll my eyes. "He was irritating, entitled, very funny, very *not* funny at all, and the kind of charming chauvinist we all should avoid."

Jody beams. "Wow, he really made an impression. So when's the wedding?"

"Shut up," I say, pressing my palms against my forehead. "You know I don't have time for some belittling romance, and I don't need a man and his backward ideas of chaining me to the kitchen floor so I can cook, clean, and be within arm's reach of the refrigerator at all times in case he wants something else to eat."

A look of understanding crosses Samantha's face. "I know the feeling."

Jody folds her arms and smirks. "Do I detect some bitterness?"

Both Samantha and I shoot her a scolding glance. I smack her hand as if administering discipline. "I'd call it being careful."

She looks at me without flinching. "I'd call it missing an opportunity. If you don't snatch him up, then I will." Her eyes pierce mine, searching for honesty.

I shake my head swiftly. "You can have him. He's not my type."

Jody grins defiantly. "You don't have a type. You have a wish list of impossibilities."

I sigh and glance away. "Worried about getting hurt, that's all."

We sit in silence for a moment. I hear the boisterous voices of the young couple seated behind me and the elderly couple seated behind Jody. Overhead, I hear Elvis now busy broadcasting how shook up he is. A waitress scoots over to our table on roller skates, holding a tray of three tall chocolate milkshakes topped with whipped cream and cherries.

"Here you go, ladies," she says cheerily, putting the breaks on her skates, handing out the magic medicine in the glasses, and scooting back to the kitchen.

Without a word, we snatch up the straws she has dropped onto the table and rip open the paper wrapping tenaciously. Moments later, our faces are pressed close to the whipped cream as we suck down the goodness which works like a narcotic.

Jody is the first to surface. Leaning back and breathing a contented sigh, she smiles mischievously. "So, Cindy, you were telling us about your future husband."

I keep my lips fastened to the straw and pretend to be looking down at the table.

Samantha tugs on my arm. "Let's have it, Cindy. No more secrets. How do you really feel about him?"

I taste the chocolate splendor pausing on my tongue before I let it slide down and make room for another mouthful. Wearing my best thoughtful expression, I rest my elbows on the table edge and lean my chin against my folded hands.

"It was uncomfortable being there with him. I'm sure he knows what he's doing, but his methods are bizarre and unnerving.

He kept diffusing tension with jokes, and he seemed insistent that I be fully aware of how hard he was working to keep me relaxed. Trying too hard, you know? But, at the same time, it was oddly effortless for him. He's an unorganized wretch, that's for certain. I only owe him a half hour more, so that's all I'm giving him. If he thinks he can find something wrong with me or try to reduce my stress by using techniques I already teach, he's a fool. A fool who's not as good-looking as he should be, but—" I catch myself and my voice trails off.

Jody and Samantha lean closer, enthralled.

"But what?" Jody exclaims.

"But he's almost not handsome enough so that he's kind of handsome. Does that make sense?"

Samantha shakes her head, perplexed. "Not really."

Jody nods vigorously. "Absolutely. I date guys like that all the time. They're less threatening. You owe it to yourself to give this guy a chance. A chance with him that doesn't work out is better than the no chance you're giving every other guy you meet."

I scratch my fingers on the table, sip some more chocolate magic, and exhale slowly. "Thirty minutes. That's all he's got. If there isn't a spark in the next session, then I'm gone and I'll be coming back to reprise my role as the ice queen for good."

"Nice," Jody replies, grinning.

"Good for you, Cindy," Samantha adds, patting my shoulder.

We glance around the '50s diner, taking in the nostalgic sights and sounds. Darkness clouds my thoughts, but I resist its compulsive pull and force a smile back onto my face, not allowing the ladies to perceive the ongoing struggle waging within me.

"I love how this place hasn't changed since we started coming here," I say, hoping to focus on the sense of escapism that the diner provides.

Jody laughs. "You'd think we'd have figured ourselves out a little more since we've frequented the joint once a week for ten years."

Samantha grins. "I'm just glad we're not your patients anymore. You're good, but milkshakes and friends are therapeutic too."

I nod eagerly. "Yep, you guys cured my anti-social ways. If I were still counseling you, I don't think we could be friends."

"Too messy?" Jody offers.

We exchange smiles. "Too personal and too deep," I answer, darting my eyes to the table. "It's easier this way."

"Sure," says Jody.

"I agree," Samantha chimes in.

Looking up, I see their averting eyes disagree. A pregnant pause drifts by as we sip our milkshakes and lose ourselves in the atmosphere of the worry-free '50s once more.

"Anyway, on a different subject, how have you been feeling?" Jody questions, still not making eye contact.

*Don't go there, Cindy. Keep leaving it alone.*

"Fine. I'm totally fine," I answer, offering the fakest smile I can muster, hoping they will believe it.

\*\*\*

Clods of dirt fling from my heels, landing harmlessly on the earthen trail behind me. My chest inhales and exhales in steady bursts. Gleaming sweat covers my skin, clinging as a reminder of precious pounds being shed. The burning exertion in my swollen feet remains unheeded as I propel myself forward. While my arms swing in fluid motion, coinciding with my fervent steps, freedom invigorates my senses, willing me to follow the weaving path ahead.

The wooded park lies on the outskirts of town, secluded from regular traffic. The main trail begins at Earl's Grocery Mart parking lot adjacent to the town's main road, but I never take the main trail. One Saturday several years ago, I discovered this tangent trail diverging away from town, a winding course without mile markers or location signs. This is my trail, the one on which I have never seen another soul.

The churning in my lungs aches with the passing miles. My black shorts flap against my thighs, and my hunter green T-shirt hugs my torso, drenched with perspiration. I can feel the redness in my cheeks and the residue of tears under my eyelids.

*Keep moving, Cindy, keep moving. Don't stop, don't rest, don't think. Just run. Just keep running away.*

While reaching up to wipe sweat from the bridge of my nose, I stray for a moment in my sight line along the trail. At first I intend to continue rushing forward, but something within me harnesses my legs to a halt. My eyes peer closely at a familiar zig-zagging path leading away from the trail to a patch of dense undergrowth. I step cautiously toward the tangled mess of ferns, umbrella plants, and fallen branches. Past the thicket mass, the path opens onto a grassy hillside. After carefully navigating the undergrowth, I arrive on the grassy spread beyond.

A thick, iron black gate stands as a threshold guardian protecting a massive graveyard resting behind it. The grassy area stretches out with a myriad of weather-worn tombstones. I unlatch the rusted lock, pry open the squeaking door, and step into the graveyard, finding a winding path of gravel chinking under my intrusive feet.

As I move further across the eerily still landscape, I observe the hillside beginning to slope with a rolling curve. The slant leads down to the end of the graveyard, where the other side of the black gate blocks the exit with a bulky metal lock. Beyond the black gate waits a narrow, mostly overgrown path, which used to lead cars through the woods to the gravesite, until the new gravesite on the other side of town sprang up a few years ago. Now this silent site is all but a forgotten relic.

I follow the gravel path to the bottom of the hill, taking in the aura around me, which resonates with powerful emptiness. My eyes rest on two lonely gravestones positioned near the edge of the graveyard, unable to escape their eternal side by side existence. The first stone, standing tall and resolute, reads *Elaine James 1913-1976*. The second stone, overshadowed and half the height of the first stone, reads *Lisa James 1940-1985*. The sight of the stones next to each other stiffens my body. Closing my eyes, I expel a shaky breath. I want to be thinking of Mama, finding some sense of solace settling upon me, but anxiety swells within me instead.

With a swift motion, I turn back toward the top of the hill, fixing my eyes on the main entrance gate of escape. Hurried steps usher me out of the graveyard and beyond the tangled undergrowth. Once I find myself secure on my trail, I sprint forward, seeking distance between myself and the haunting presence weighing on my mind like an engraved stone jutting up from the grassy earth.

***

The final rays of sun dip below the tree line.   Darkness consumes the house for its nightly dominance.  I make the necessary preparations: locking the outer doors, closing curtains, and lighting candles.

At last, I change into my nightgown and complete my nightly bathroom ritual.   Tonight, however, I find myself gazing in the mirror for an unusually long time, scowling at my too-narrow nose, too-short eyelashes, too-numerous freckles, too-pale skin, and too-prevalent wrinkles.  Ugly face, ugly body—nothing worth looking at. I long to see the confident Cindy I saw in my dreams the other night, but she is nowhere to be found in my reflection.  After making another dissatisfied face at myself, I flick off the bathroom light and trudge into the bedroom.

Before climbing into bed, I slink over to the window, pull back the curtain, and lift one of the blinds to see into the moonlit backyard.  I imagine a womanly figure creeping around near the back fence line, trying to find an opening where she can escape. The figure does not turn to look up at me, but I know she is watching me, just as I am watching out for her.

Then I blink and realize there is no huddled woman scavenging in the moonlight.  There is only a scar of land tilled up where a lush garden once grew.  A smattering of wrought iron archways lay stacked against each other at the edge of the back deck. The remains of a gazebo and a tool shed lay hacked into firewood, neatly piled in uniform rows across from the archway pile.  Several wheelbarrows adjacent to the woodpile are filled with shattered stone plant pot and statue piece remains, resting undisturbed since the day they were brought into the backyard.  Giant weeds have overtaken the grass, sprouting up with unsightly prowess.  Even the fence line, nearly one hundred yards away from the back wall of the house, wears the marks of disrepair and weathered aging.

A mental image flashes in my mind, a picture of a girl seeing this same backyard alive with vibrant colors and tantalizing scents. I feel that I do not know this girl and do not remember why anything except the weed-infested, beauty-less area I see before me ever existed.

I release the raised blind and retrieve the long-nosed lighter from the dresser, adding a flame to the candle beside the window. Then I crawl into bed and my eyes close gradually.

My eyes open to a graveyard. Endless tombstones in my vision rest in peaceful slumber. Gravel crunches beneath my feet. My cheeks feel the biting brush of the air's chill and my foggy breath expels weighty wisps. I glance down to see I am covered only in my nightgown.

With an unsteady swallow, I begin moving down the hillside to the bottom of the graveyard. Sprinkling mist settles on me, as if tasting and testing my form for purity. The headstone markers, silent in solitude, pass by as I pass on with numbed motion. I glimpse the thick black gate standing resolutely at the end of the graveyard, locked and disallowing exit.

Upon reaching the base of the hillside, I expect to find two tombstones side by side, one belonging to Elaine James and the other belonging to Lisa James, but their stones are nowhere in sight. Instead, two new grave markers stand in their place. The first stone is miniscule, scarcely more than a fist-sized marker, below which lies the wrinkled picture of a smiling young girl. The marker reads *Cindy Jeanetta 1960-1973*. My eyes move to the next stone, a larger, rectangular marker, below which lies the picture of a headless woman. The picture is seamless and appears to have been carefully maintained. The marker reads *Ms. James 1973-present*.

The mist turns to rain as I stand rigidly, my eyes absorbing the scene. The water splashes across my forehead and pounds against my shoulders, but it remains unfelt. I bend down to sit on the rough gravel—hoping the rain will wash me away completely—and close my eyes, dissolving into darkness.

My arms and legs tremble erratically as I awaken. I slide further down in the bed, feeling my feet hanging off the edge. Following a deep breath, I pull the covers over my head and lay unmoving, waiting for the thumping of my heart to subside.

# *Chapter Five*

My shaking fingers rotate the keys to turn off the car's engine. The sensation of my lungs trying to force my breath to quicken in hyperventilating gasps causes sharp pain in my chest. I place a hand below my sternum, trying to steady my slightly heaving torso and concentrate on deep breathing.

*Just thirty minutes, Cindy. Only half an hour and you'll be ready to return to work. Thirty minutes, that's all. You've had ice cream binges that have lasted longer. You can do this.*

The rush of swirling April wind funnels into the vehicle as I step out of the car. Once again, the worn and torn Pontiac Grand Am, still decorated in a fine coat of wind-pressed dirt, sits two spots over in the parking lot. Resisting the compulsion to scurry around to the driver's side, smash the window, break in to hot wire the engine, and scoot the bucket of bolts off to the nearest car wash, I instead walk to the main entrance door with as much resolution as I can muster. I make my way inside to Tony's office door, my eyes glancing greedily at the candy dish on the reception table.

*Don't you dare put your hand in that bowl, Cindy Jeanetta James. Stay focused. You have a singular mission: get in, get him distracted, and get out. There's no time for chocolate indulgence in the midst of battle.*

I almost motion to knock when I hear him hop out of his chair and shuffle over to the door. I half-expect him to swing open the door and stand proudly like a misbehaving child with chocolate smeared across his face. Instead, I watch the door open slowly, his olive eyes peering at me curiously.

"You've come back for more chocolate, I see. You're early," he announces with amusement.

"I'm always running ahead of schedule," I reply with an apologetic smile.

"Excellent. That means I'll have more time to pick your brain and weasel out a confession. Please, come on in."

The door swings open fully and I enter cautiously. He waves his hand flippantly toward the pair of couches while closing the door. I spot the distressing sight of his cluttered desk.

*Block it out, Cindy. Block it out. Remember, it's his desk, not yours.*

I close my eyes strenuously while pausing on my way to the couch against the right wall. When my eyes open again, I notice I have arrested his fascinated gaze.

"And to what do I owe the pleasure of seeing that splendid aversion reaction? Is it merely spending time with me, or is it the desk?"

"What?" I ask dumbly, sitting down in the exact same position on the couch where I sat during the last session. I quickly shed my coat and lay it beside my purse.

"That closed-eyes aversion thing you just did. I bet it was because of my desk. Am I right?"

My hands fumble and sweat together. "I don't know what you mean. I didn't know we had started the session yet."

He chuckles, grabs his favorite chewed up pen and notepad from his desk, and moves over to plop down on the opposite couch. "You know what I mean, Ms. James. I saw you mash your eyelids together to block out something that was nauseating you. Personally, I would like to predict that it was the desk rather than me, but I've been wrong before."

I find myself looking down at the coffee table and giggling nervously. *What is that, Cindy? We don't giggle, especially not for this moron.* "It was nothing," I reply, almost under my breath.

He nods matter-of-factly. "It's the desk, for sure. So what about the desk in particular troubles you? Is it the mountain of unorganized paper chaos? Or is it the chewed pens?"

"It's nothing," I insist adamantly.

"Ms. James, you take me to be a foolish slob. In actuality, I'm only a slob. I could tell the appearance of my office bothered you the last time you were here. You even needed chocolate to ease the trauma. So, which is it, the papers or the pens?"

I cross my arms, sigh heavily, and look him straight in the eyes. "It's everything, Mr. Prost. It's the entire desk with every last piece of untidy paper strewn across it. It's the two coffee stains on your floor directly between your loveseat and the desk, where your must sip your morning coffee in between notations, seeing that you are right-handed. It's the chocolates and how you keep pushing them like a drug dealer. It's your whole demeanor and your approach to counseling, like this is a party and we're just hanging out over drinks and chocolates. That's what bothers me, Mr. Prost. I know you are probably certified to do this kind of work, based on the degrees you've told me you have, but you haven't shown me anything to make me believe that you know what you're doing in the slightest."

A moment passes—more of an impasse than an awkward silence. Then he smiles. "Very good, Ms. James. You've just made up for the entire get-to-know-you session that we were supposed to have last time. Now we're all caught up, so we can dig deeper and see what really ticks you off. I'm sorry, what really makes you tick."

His eyes are resilient, daring me to banter. "I know where you're going with this, Mr. Prost, and it's not going to work. We've already wasted almost fifteen minutes of my time, so you only have fifteen minutes left and then you'll never see me again."

He smirks. "I don't plan on ever seeing you again. In fact, I'm hoping for it."

I lean back, ruffled, lost for words. He takes in my stunned expression, unfazed.

"You are far too uptight for my taste, Ms. James. You have all of the answers, and you clearly don't want my questions. My time would be better spent working with a patient who actually wants to get better."

His last statement resonates with a strange panging sensation. I expel a frustrated sigh and shake my head pointedly. "You don't even know me, Mr. Prost, so don't judge me. My personal business is none of your professional business."

He tosses the notepad and gnawed pen onto the coffee table and begins drumming his fingers on his kneecaps. "Very well, no notes, no recording, no expectations. If you think I'm such a terrible therapist, then I want you to take the final fourteen minutes of time that we will ever spend together and explain to me why you believe you don't need help and why I am the worst person to give you the help you assume you don't need."

"Look, Mr. Prost—"

"Please call me Tony," he interrupts. "I find it unprofessional to be called by anything other than my informal name."

I give him a smirk. "As I was saying, Mr. Prost, I'm not going to play this game with you. You'll want to examine my significant stressors, my hidden feelings, my childhood traumas, all the backward ways of thinking I have about myself and others. You'll try to locate the transposed expectations, whether actual or perceived, the categorical assumptions I make about what 'should' be done or who 'should' or 'should not' do it. Don't play me for stupid, Mr. Prost, and don't patronize me. The jokes, the chocolates, the chewed pens, the scatter-brained mad scientist persona, the tornado alley office space, the light-hearted quipping—it's merely an elaborate gimmick to ply results from me. Well, I'm not giving in to your sugar-filled truth serum and easy-going charm."

He is momentarily speechless, raising an eyebrow with keen interest. "You're absolutely right, Ms. James. You've made it perfectly clear that I'm the one with issues, not you. It appears, based on your keen analysis, that I'm unorganized and messy beyond repair, I lure women with chocolates to my therapy lair, and, apparently, I have charm. Not bad for a guy who has no clue what he's doing. Now you've answered the second part of my question of why I'm not qualified to help you. So, with only eleven minutes left in our turbulent relationship, I want to know the first part. Why do you believe you don't need help at all?"

Without warning me ahead of time, my eyes close. The vision flashes across my mind of the girl hiding beneath her bed, shielding her ears with her hands. I picture myself lying on the red room floor, clutching headless Raggedy Ann close to me as my tears puddle on the floor. I see the graveyard and my two gravestones side by side, wishing they could be washed away by the rain.

I open my eyes and stare at the quirky man waiting patiently on the opposite couch. His eyes are glued to mine.

"I do need help," I say softly, "but I don't need a therapist."

My eyes widen in shock at my words. The surprise swells within his expression as well, although he fights to conceal it.

"Okay, Ms. James. If you need help, but you don't need a therapist, then what is it you *really* need?"

My sweaty hands are shaking. I slide them under my thighs to pin them down. I feel flushed, almost feverish. After a deep breath for assurance, I look at him squarely.

"I need a friend. Just a friend who will talk with me. Someone who can actually understand. Just a friend, that's all."

He sighs and smiles. "That's quite a tall order. A friend who can actually understand you? A rare quality indeed. Mind if I give it a try?"

"What?" I ask, feeling the burning irritation of water in my eyes.

"Can I be your friend? Obviously, we've established that I'm not sufficiently qualified to be your therapist, so can I take a stab at being that person you described who will talk with you, who will actually understand you, who will be your 'just a friend, that's all'? How about it? Will you give me the chance to make up for my utter failure as your therapist?"

A smile sneaks across my mouth against my better judgment. "But we don't even know each other, Mr. Prost."

His eyes dance. "Hence, the agreement to become friends. That initiates the process whereby we stop making cutting remarks about each other's therapy techniques and/or lack of organizational skills and the process whereby we start truly talking to each other." He smiles, inviting me to relax within myself.

"Okay," I say tentatively.

"Well, I must demand that you stop calling me Mr. Prost. It makes me feel like my father, who was a far better therapist and man than I'll ever be. From now on, it's either Tony or friend, nothing else, please."

I offer a simple smile, which strikes me as oddly unburdening. "All right."

He hops off the couch and extends his hand. We shake hands and then he releases me. "Looks like our thirty minutes are up. I won't make you come back here anymore to see the cluttered desk madness. What do you say we meet for lunch to talk as 'just friends'? How about the '50s diner on Friday at noon? I went there for the first time last week and it's going to be a staple for me now. Have you ever been there?"

I nod. "Yes, I've been there."

"So I'll see you soon, Cindy."

"Okay, Tony," I say, gathering up my purse and jacket.

He opens the door and smiles as I make my way into the hallway.

"Have a marvelous afternoon," he says, tossing me a Hershey's Kiss which must have been hidden in his pocket.

I catch the piece firmly in my hand and smile back at him. "Good-bye."

As I leave the building and come to my car, I grip the chocolate in my fingers while mulling over the bizarre realization of having just entered into a verbal contract of friendship with the same man I was hell-bent on never seeing again only thirty minutes ago.

# *Chapter Six*

I find myself seated across from Tony Prost at the '50s diner table. His face reminds me why I should not have initially categorized him as unhandsome. Has his face changed since our first meeting, has it actually grown more handsome? Am I seeing him differently now that we are supposedly "just friends"?

*It's the loneliness speaking, Cindy. Shut it down and don't give any credence to attraction. You don't want to end up like Mama.*

I thumb the edge of my napkin while keeping my gaze locked on the tabletop. His penetrating stare is turning my face what I'm sure is a hideous shade of red. This was a terrible idea meeting here, meeting at all.

*How long does it take to cook a hamburger? Are they back there in the kitchen butchering the cow?*

"You're pensive today," he says. "Are you already over-analyzing our getting together for lunch?"

I dare to meet his gaze. "I'm just tired," I mutter, half-smiling.

Without warning, he extends his hand across the table toward me, not quite touching my hand. "You can relax, you know. Not every guy is threatening."

"I'm not threatened," I reply, feeling my jaw tighten.

"I haven't known you very long, but I can tell that you're put off by men. Is it men's arrogance, their ignorance, or all of the above? Present company excluded, of course." He offers a smile.

I choose not to reciprocate the smile. "I'm not put off by men. I believe what I have is called discretion. I've spent a total of an hour and ten minutes with you, so how do I even know anything about you? Besides, I thought our agreement was to be 'just friends'? If you have something else in mind, I'll be taking my burger to go."

He holds up his hands in self-defense. "No ulterior motives, I promise. I only want the opportunity to learn a little more about you, so I can fully understand the extent to which I'll never figure you out."

I smirk at him. "Do you usually take female patients out to lunch?"

"Only the hyper-sensitive, neurotic ones."

I fold my arms and stare him down. "I bet all of your patients leave more confused about themselves than they were when they walked into your office. I thought you were clueless and charming before, but now I see you are intentionally smug."

His eyes darken a bit, a new glance from his arsenal. "Do the jokes not work for you? Perhaps if I demanded confessions by force, then you'd like me better? Or maybe I should play the aloof introvert who jots notes and pretends to be piecing together some mental puzzle? I happen to be a very good therapist because I don't try to come across like a therapist. Sorry if my non-uptight, productive methods bother you. I suppose my casual methodology grates against your controlling sensibilities."

I lean back in my seat, ruffled. "Tell me, how many weak-willed women has your routine worked on? Do you always sucker them in with chocolate, or does each new town require a different sugar tranquilizer?"

He shakes his head, smiling wryly. "I don't know. I've never tried it before. You were the first. Although I should have chosen a less irritable subject to study. So, did the chocolate work on you?"

I roll my eyes. "Conceited jerk," I say, mostly under my breath.

"Beautiful witch," he replies, mostly under his breath.

We stare at each other, mutually stunned.

"What did you call me?" I stammer, wide-eyed.

He allows the unnerving pause to settle in until it becomes agonizing. Then he smiles sincerely. "I called you beautiful."

I am lost for words, scrambling in my thoughts for a direction. He takes my silence in stride and leans forward, more desperate than aggressive. "Look, Cindy, I'm just a little miffed that you're stone-walling me for something I didn't even do."

His face strikes me as acutely handsome, growing in appeal as the argument increases in intensity.

*Shut it down, Cindy. You know where that leads.*

"And what's that?"

"Not totally sure," he replies thoughtfully, "but it's either a disastrous guy relationship from the past or some deep-seated daddy issue, I'm guessing."

I sense my eyes swelling with momentary vulnerability, followed by sharp anger. "I think this concludes our bad-decision friendship."

I make a motion to stand from my seat, but he reaches his hand across the table and places it on my hand. The sensation of his skin on mine is both electrifying and terrifying. The nerves in my hand tingle with jarring fervor. The throbbing of my heart quickens its pace. I look in his eyes and see an endearing brokenness.

"I'm sorry, Cindy. I was just provoking you. Pseudo-conflict, you know? I thought it would spice things up. Please don't leave."

*He's using you, Cindy. Don't give in to his act. Run now before you're snared.*

My body stiffens and my eyes grow cold. "Please let go of my hand."

He withdraws his hand, although his eyes maintain their plea for help. "Sorry, I wanted to try to understand you. I see now it was a mistake for me to believe that you are anything but unforgiving and unfeeling." His tone is melancholy.

I find myself leaning forward unexpectedly. "Why do you do that?" His eyes are distant, confused. "You approach me as if I'm some unfixable woman who holds the key to your sense of accomplishment, if only you could unravel my mystery. Don't treat me like I'm damaged. I'm not your patient, I'm not your friend, and I'm definitely not your woman. Are we done here?"

He nods with resignation. "I don't think you're fixable, and I don't think you're unfixable. You're only a person hiding, and I bet you're running out of people who will want to keep seeking you out. You need more than therapy, Cindy; you need a real life, the life that's hidden beneath these false layers of the perfect person you want to believe you are."

I scowl at him. "I'm the only credible therapist here. Take your gimmicks, your chocolates, and your male bravado, and go sell your cotton candy therapy to someone else. You can make your patients laugh and foolishly believe you can help them, but in the end, you'll just leave them despairing and wanting to kill themselves."

He stares at me, stone-faced. He rummages in his pocket without removing his eyes from me. Two twenty-dollar bills appear in his hand and he tosses them onto the table. He slides out of the booth, stands up swiftly, and walks out of the diner.

Moments after he is gone, the sound of cheery chatter from the surrounding booths, as well as Elvis paying tribute to a hound dog, fills my ears. The strange tingling sensation pricks my legs and arms like dozens of knitting needles. The chipper blonde waitress swings around the corner, hoisting a tray supporting two plates, each with a greasy hamburger and side of French fries. She scoots to the table and lowers the plates onto the checkered top.

"Here you go," her high-pitched voice grates in my ears. "Will that be all, or would you two like anything else?"

I glance up at her beaming face and offer a sad smile. "No, that's all for us, thanks."

***

*Mama, I need to talk to you. It's a guy issue. Yes, it's about that one named Tony again. I'm fairly positive the most likable quality about him— which, of course, is the characteristic I most despise—is his ability to speak something that is true about me without regret, caution, or tact.*

*The main problem is that I feel drawn to him, though I want nothing more than to keep him away from me. I want him to hear what I have to say, but I also want to hurt him enough to warn him to be mindful of the distance I need. Is there something wrong with me? Why is every motive and method I have organized for myself two-faced?*

*I can tell I have wounded him. There's some secret he's holding, and he seems insistent on staying hidden as much as he claims I am. Should I apologize to him? Would that only leave me exposed as an easier target in the future? Why do I even care if I gave him a few bruises? He brought them on himself.*

*Yes, I know what I need to do. Don't think for a moment that I'll be foolish enough to care about this man. He doesn't deserve my care, because I can't afford additional scars, the inevitable let down at the end of anything we would begin. There's no possible way I'm going to call him to apologize. Goodnight, Mama.*

I fumble in the darkness, brushing my hand against the alarm clock which reads 2 a.m., before flipping on the lamp switch. With frustration, I seize my address book and phone receiver, wrestling its connective cord into submission. My weary eyes scroll down the address list until arriving at the entry labeled *CBT Guy*. I dial the number and wait for the incessant ringing tone, cringing inside. After several rings, his recorded voice echoes in my ear.

"This is Tony Prost with Tony Prost Cognitive Behavioral Therapy. Please leave your name, your number, and a detailed message, and I will return your call as soon as possible. Have a great day."

The jarring beep sounds and I am left with a void of silence to fill.

*This is where it would have been a bright idea to prepare your statement ahead of time, Cindy. How unorganized is this? Very out of character for you. What's going on in your head?*

"Um, hi, Tony. This is Cindy. I know it's late, but I wanted to say—"

Suddenly, a crackling sound interrupts the line. "This is Tony," he says groggily, followed by a yawn.

My eyes grow wide, as a lump in my throat feels caught, rendering me speechless.

"Hello?" his offbeat voice resonates in my ear. "Is that you, Cindy?"

"Yes—" I stammer, feeling my heart thumping in my chest.

"Do you know what time it is? Are you okay?" He waits for my response. "You still there?"

"I'm here, and yes, I'm fine," I say softly, shakily. "I just wanted to apologize."

"Apologize? Oh, for me being insensitive at the diner this afternoon? Yes, I wanted to apologize for that too. I'm glad we're in agreement."

It takes several moments for me to gather my thoughts. "No, that's not what I meant. I wanted to apologize for how I behaved, for what I said."

I wait for his voice to return, sensing my heart beating so rapidly that I worry he will hear it over the phone.

"Hmm," he mumbles thoughtfully. "I don't seem to remember anything you said that requires an apology. So, if you'll do me the courtesy of forgiving my brutish behavior, we can get on with our lives.  Sound fair?"

"But I don't understand."  I hear wretched panic in my voice. The weak, pleading tone is hideous.

*Don't be needy, Cindy.  Let him off the hook before you get hooked.*

He sighs.  "So do you forgive me?"

"I guess so, but—"

"Good, then I'll see you tomorrow."

The phone line clicks as he hangs up.  I wait for a few moments for him to call back, but when the phone remains silent, I place the receiver back onto the base and deposit the address book beside it.  Then I slink beneath the covers and struggle for another several hours to find sleep.

# Chapter Seven

I sit alone in the '50s diner, letting my mind drift—a habit that usually takes a turn for the dangerous. The veneer of lively chatter buzzing about scarcely makes a dent in my consciousness. The only reality is my fingers scratching the checker top table.

My thoughts move to Mama, another dangerous habit. I search for her face in my daydreaming, but her image is murky, like a drowning victim's profile being distorted by churning water. I wonder what she would think of the compulsions that have been passed down to me: Raggedy Ann, the red room, the chronic cleaning—these wretched masterpieces of mine of which she was partially the maker. If only I could reconcile the sane Cindy with the one I fear will give in to the same fate as Mama, the madness maker. Fending off this paranoia of possibly discovering that her disease has infected me is a full-time occupation. Will I become another victim to the plague befalling the James women, helplessly watching sanity depart from me with a mocking, clownish grin?

*Don't taunt me, Mama. I'm doing my best to keep it together. You didn't do such a good job yourself.*

My fingers cease their compulsive scratching. I cup my hands on my elbows and hunch against the tabletop. It is alone times like these that bring the agonizing *what ifs* full circle. What if I slip and accidentally reveal to Jody or Samantha what actually goes on in my house on a nightly basis? What if I disclose my bizarre behaviors to Tony while undergoing his unorthodox interrogation? What if I remain alone and unloved, unprotected from the darkest danger that could possibly capture me: myself? What if my mind clouds like a fog that never breaks, blurring the line between normalcy and insanity until it becomes something I can no longer distinguish? What if the curse has already been passed on to me from Mama—

that horrible disintegration of dignity, that collapse of control over self—coming to consume my blood, my body, my brain?

*You'll never be normal, Cindy. There's no hope for your mind to stay together. Just like Mama's, just like Grandma's, it will scatter like a bucket of marbles being dumped onto the floor, rolling away, impossible to gather up every one of them.*

*You lie, Cindy. I refuse to listen to your pessimism. You only want to twist my thoughts against me. I don't want to lose my mind, the one thing that anchors me to who I am.*

*You may not have a choice. I know your defenses will wear down in time.*

*Get away from me. Your depressive brooding is draining.*

*You can't fight me forever. Sooner or later you'll give in and lose your grip.*

*I am sane, Cindy. I will always be sane. You can't take me away.*

*I am insane, Cindy. So are you. So are we. Get it? Your mind is corruptible, just like anything else. All we need is the right push to tip you over the edge and into the abyss.*

*I'm still a normal woman.*

*You're still a broken woman.*

*I can change.*

*No one believes you can change, especially not you and me. So chew it up and chat it up at the '50s diner, avoiding the darkness stirring inside. Fake your happiness for them, just like you've been doing all these years. See if they keep falling for it as easily as you do.*

*I'll keep fighting you. You won't control me.*

*Sweet, stupid Cindy. You'll never learn. You'll give in to the darkness. It's only a matter of time.*

"Well, you're looking downright depressed!" Jody's upbeat voice blasts my ears like a siren.

Flinching, I look up and see Jody, Samantha, and a pretty blonde lady staring at me, startled.

"Oh, sorry, just daydreaming," I mutter, prying my elbows off the table and scooting across the bench to the far corner to make room.

"Pile in, ladies," Jody announces, gracefully withholding any jabbing remarks about the content of my daydreaming.

Within moments, the four of us are snug in the booth, trading greeting glances.

Samantha, seated beside me, motions to the pretty blonde. "Cindy, this is my friend, Bridget, who I was telling you about."

"Glad you could join us," I offer, reaching across the tabletop to shake her hand.

"I've heard so much about you," Bridget replies with a picture perfect smile, showcasing her jealousy-inducing pearly whites.

"I wouldn't believe the majority of it," I say, shyly smiling.

"Don't be modest, Cindy," Jody quips with a smirk. "You're the best of us and you know it."

"Anyway—" I begin, desperate for a topic change. "I think I'm ready to go back to work later this week."

The mouths of Jody and Samantha drop open, incredulous.

"Are you kidding?" Jody snaps.

"No, I'm fine," I insist.

"Fine enough to stay home and rest up," Jody counters.

Samantha pats my arm. "You need to take it easy, Cindy."

I sigh abruptly. "I need to feel normal again. Working will help bring me back to center, you know?"

Samantha shakes her head. "But is it safe? Aren't you still having symptoms?"

"I'm fine," I reply hastily. "I'm totally fine. No issues at all."

Even as I speak, my hands hide beneath the table, my left hand trying to massage the spasm out of my right hand.

"So, Bridget," I say, pasting on a smile. "You must be bored with this conversation. How did you end up here in Sleepy Oak?"

"Well—" she begins, launching into a detailed explanation that passes into one ear and out of the other for me.

*Focus, Cindy. If you're going to get well, then you need to make sure no one has any doubts that you are well. You can't afford to lose patients or friends—or respect. You've got this. Just work past it in your mind, and then you'll be able to work past it in your body. If you keep convincing yourself that you're normal, then you just might have a chance of becoming that way. Show no weakness, no compulsions. Keep smiling, that's it. Show those teeth, just as pearly white as this new girl's. The ladies are buying the act, so stay chipper and they'll stay clueless. We need this. Don't disappoint me.*

Bridget's voice crescendos in my ears. "So that's why I ended up settling down in Sleepy Oak. Isn't that crazy?"

I smile and nod eagerly. "The craziest," I say, making solid eye contact with her, which she perceives as an act of approval on my part.

A perky waitress scoots up on her skates. "What'll it be, ladies?"

Jody waves her hand in a wide circle. "Four chocolate shakes with extra chocolate, extra whipped cream, extra cherries, and some more extra chocolate. Actually, make that five shakes, in case I want seconds."

"Comin' up," replies the waitress before veering away toward the kitchen.

Bridget rests a hand on the table in neutral territory between us, careful not to advance too far to my side. "Samantha tells me you're a therapist."

"Most days," I answer, glancing away.

"What kind of therapy do you do?" she persists.

"Well, I'm a cognitive behavioral therapist—" I begin hesitantly.

Jody picks up my pause and graciously intervenes. "She's a life solver, plain and simple."

I roll my eyes.

"Seriously," Jody insists. "Stress management, self-perceptions, breathing techniques, healthy communication principles—she does it all. Samantha and I used to be patients, and if it wasn't for Cindy, we'd still be pulling our hair out and crying ourselves to sleep at night."

Bridget's eyes grow wide. "That sounds dramatic."

Jody smiles. "No joke." Then, strangely, she looks at her watch and half-smiles. "Say, while we wait for the milkshakes, why don't we talk about relationships?"

I give her a suspicious glance. "Why?"

Suddenly, my eyes peer above Jody's face with a mix of amazement, embarrassment, and terror. Tony Prost marches over to our table, flaunting the largest grin he owns. He is wearing the rugged red flannel shirt and weathered blue jeans again.

"Sorry I'm late," he says, offering a fake humble chuckle of nervousness. "What did I miss?"

I stare at him, speechless. He stands waiting for my response, enjoying the reaction he must have certainly predicted.

"Come on in, mister," Jody chirps, nudging Bridget into the corner and patting the seat next to her. "We're just getting started."

He nods and sweeps into the booth, diagonal from me. Unfazed, his eyes survey the four women taking stock of him. The other ladies appear to be fawning young girls drawn like gullible moths to a schmuck of a flame. Their faces are glowing, awed at the sight of this peculiar male creature who has invaded our sanctuary.

"I met Tony the other day at the pharmacy," Jody announces, "and I thought he could use some good female company since he's new in town."

Tony blushes with fake humility. "Hi, I'm Tony."

"I'm Samantha."

"I'm Bridget."

"I'm—I'm—uh—you know—Cindy—"

"Are you sure?" he asks, smiling peevishly.

I watch their eyes being hypnotized by his unhandsome face.

*Are they seeing a different man in the room than I am? Put an end to this, Cindy; don't let it get out of control.*

"So," Jody says, rubbing her hands together with anticipation. "We were just going to start talking about relationships. Wanna join in?"

Tony shrugs. "Sure, why not? A fair warning, I don't have much advice to give in that area."

Jody elbows him playfully. "No worries. Nothing's off limits at the diner. Cindy, do you want to start us off?"

Redness flares in my cheeks. "Oh—no—I don't have anything to say."

"That'll be a first," Tony says with a chuckle. "I don't know if you ladies are aware, but I'm actually a cognitive behavioral therapist myself, and I've been going to Cindy for counseling. She has wonderful insights and she's helping me through some issues."

The ladies' eyes turn to me. I see him wink at me discreetly before I avert my eyes to the tabletop. "That's not exactly true—"

"Please, share your wisdom with us," Tony challenges, his tone buoyant and edging on flirtatious.

I sense the trembling in my right hand wanting to erupt in an uncontrollable tremor.

*He's like a rabid dog, Cindy. Feed him a treat, lure him into a cage, and then put him down and out of your misery.*

"Seriously, I have nothing to share," I say softly. "Why don't you tell us about yourself, Tony? Surely you have plenty of relationship stories from before you moved here."

His face shines resplendently. "Well, thank you ladies for allowing me to intrude on your party, but honestly, I don't have much to offer on that subject."

"Fine, I'll start," Jody interjects, extending her hands between us as if calming quarreling lovers. "You two are awfully tongue-tied for being therapists who speak to people all day long."

Tony grins at me and I glare at him.

"Anyway," Jody continues, "finding love is stressful. The standard rules of relationships don't work for me. I want to know someone loves me by the time the first date is done. That's where I get in hot water. Most men want things to stay casual and run their non-committal course. But the ones who might be interested in something more serious come with a laundry list of demands. I'm not too fond of being tied down by some man's expectations. Tony, what do you think?"

He glances at me curiously and then looks back at her. "I don't know—"

"Oh, come on," Jody says, smacking his arm as she might a younger brother's. "You're a therapist. Fix me."

He laughs and folds his arms. "Well, love's not that simple. Relationships are complicated by definition."

Jody rolls her eyes. "Enough clichés, doc. Give it to me like a shot in the arm."

He sighs and sweeps his gaze from face to face, landing on mine considerably longer than the others. "I think it's natural to want to find love. Perhaps your perceived expectation of what a man is concluding about you from the first date is setting you up for disappointment. After all, you mentioned that you don't want to be tied down by unwanted expectations, but it seems there may be a double standard at work. You believe the man to be capable and responsible for making a long-term decision based on a one-time encounter, a decision that could be construed by him as an unwanted expectation. Maybe if you gave him more time to get to know you before giving him the axe, he could realize how much he might enjoy the type of non-standard relationship you've been craving."

A pregnant pause waddles across the table.

"You're good," Jody says, blushing.

Seeming emboldened, Bridget leans forward and gazes intently at Tony. "I've also had troubles with love. The stress of it for me is the whole concept of love itself. You have attraction and you have repulsion, but everything in between is a mess. How do you know when you've arrived at love? What does it feel like? How can you reduce your stress about finding love while still actively searching for it?"

"Well—" Tony begins.

"Actually," I interject, scrambling for a diversion. *Put down the dog, Cindy. He's spreading rabies to the ladies. You've fed him and brought him into the cage. Now finish the deed and move on.* "This is sounding too much like a therapy session. I thought we were just friends getting together for casual conversation."

This time Samantha interrupts me. "Actually, Cindy, if you don't mind, I would like to hear Tony's thoughts. This is helpful, I think."

Tony exudes a shy smile.

*How I loathe this man.*

"As I said, I'm hardly an expert on the subject," he says humbly. "Let's have each of you give your own thoughts first. I'm interested to see what viewpoints we're working with."

The ladies' faces illuminate with newfound purpose.

Jody jumps in first. "I think love is when you have baggage within yourself that you can't stand, and then you finally find someone who isn't bothered by it as much as you are. Someone who doesn't think of you as badly as you do, that's someone who loves you."

"Good," Tony comments, nodding with approval.

Samantha states quietly, "I think love is when you find meaning because someone is in your life. Like Carl, my husband, well, he loves me when he says my cooking isn't as terrible as it was when we first got married. When he's not drunk and he's actually sober enough to kiss me goodnight, that's when I know he loves me. Without him, I'm not a whole person, I guess. So that must be love?"

"Okay, very honest. Good," Tony says, giving her an understanding expression that she soaks up as truth.

Bridget leans toward Tony, gushing with her eyes. "I think love might be when you're willing to accept that you're not perfect and the person you're with isn't perfect either, but together, you're better because you're perfect for each other."

"Good," Tony says, and Brittany flashes him a winning smile.

All eyes swerve to me, waiting expectantly. My cheeks burn with embarrassment. The trembling in my right hand nearly causes it to strike the underside of the table, so I quickly slide my hand under my thigh.

"Oh, I don't know. Love doesn't make sense to me, because it always ends." Their eyes remain glued to my face, unyielding. *Get this under control, Cindy. You are totally out of order here.* "Okay, well, I guess I would have to say, honestly, that I think love is a painful process of impossible connection between two people. That's why I believe what we assume to be love so often fails. I may sound cynical, but in my experience, love is only a mistaken label for temporary attraction leading to unreasonable expectations, futile affections, and jarring disappointments."

The silence is deafening. The girls' eyes are stunned.

"I agree with Cindy," Tony states resolutely, breaking the agonizing tension. All eyes, including mine, dart to his face. "I think love is an impossible connection between two people, but I also think that's the beauty of it. Two people, littered with flaws, agreeing to come to terms with its inherent impossibility and choosing to stick together despite the incongruent nature of themselves. That's beautiful. At least it is to me."

They resound like a trio.

"I agree."

"Oh, yeah."

"I get that."

I am the odd woman out, staring at this man, mystified. He looks at me, as if waiting for the next directive. I feel vulnerability peeling away my resistance, betraying my weakness for a moment to his keen observation. Then, like rubble resurrecting itself into a wall, my defenses hastily raise an appropriate barrier of distance.

*No weakness, Cindy. Don't disappoint me.*

Jody waves a hand in my direction. "Cindy, tell me what you meant when you said love doesn't make sense to you because it always ends."

Their eyes swerve back to my face, scrutinizing anxiously. The threat of tears wells up as my heart careens in freefall. "I—I—"

Suddenly, my salvation arrives in the form of the waitress carrying a tray of five chocolate milkshakes. Their attention scatters as the tasty diversions are dispersed from hand to hand. The magic medicine breaks the tension and causes the four of them to mingle with each other amicably. The ladies gravitate with school-girl giddiness to the well-spoken, unhandsome yet undeniably handsome man. Between deep sips of my sweet, delicious escape—while their boisterous conversation and laughter fills the booth—I sneak in steadying breaths to calm my swirling thoughts. All the while, I continue hiding my hands beneath the table, rubbing my right hand fervently to work out the erratically twitching tremor.

\*\*\*

A high-pitched ringing reverberates from somewhere in the darkness. I lift my heavy arm over to the nightstand and retrieve the phone. The alarm clock reads 2:30 a.m. As I place the phone to my ear, I stretch my feet to the bottom edge of the bed, anxious to stifle the shaking, tingling sensation which has been crawling up and down each limb like a spider's creeping legs for the past three hours.

"This is Cindy."

"Sorry to call you so late," *CBT Guy's* voice registers.

"You owe me an apology for this afternoon," I say plainly.

His voice is chipper in my ear. "Sorry. I figured it was my only way to see you again so that we could continue our feud."

I sigh and scrunch my forehead, annoyed at the tremor in my hand that is causing the phone to shift up and down against my ear. "I don't like being blindsided."

"I figured as much. It's easier to control what you know is coming."

"I'm going to need more therapy just to recover from spending time with you," I say, feeling the heaviness coming with greater intensity, spreading like a weighty blanket across my body.

"A valid point."

I blink hard several times, trying to clear the blurred spots in my vision. "So what do you think of my friends?"

"They're fantastic. It's fascinating to me that you go to that diner with them every single week. Aren't there any other restaurants in this small town? Maybe a trendy night spot where you ladies could wine and dine?"

"The '50s diner is our ritual. I wouldn't expect you to understand."

"Hmm. How long have you known them?"

"Ten—ten—y—years," I struggle to speak. *Focus, Cindy. No weakness. Concentrate on your words.* "I first met them at the diner. They were both going through difficult times, so we started having informal therapy sessions at my house for several months. Then, after we stopped the sessions, we stayed in touch and became friends. The weekly get-together at the diner has kept us connected all these years. It's our es—es—escape—from re—reality."

"I think your phone is breaking up," he says. "So, that must have been after your time in Kansas City when you earned your degrees?"

"Yes—Jody and Samantha—hel—helped me—to—to—" A throbbing sensation erupts in my temples.

"The phone connection is bad, Cindy. What did you say?"

I open my mouth to speak, but no sound comes out. After another moment of concentrated effort, I slur together the words, "To get—away—from her—"

An awkward pause hangs in my ear. "That's not the phone, is it? Cindy, are you all right? You just sounded like you were slurring your speech. Is everything okay?"

"I'm—fine. To—tally—fine." My words are garbled and painfully slow.

*It's happening again, Cindy. Keep breathing. Deep breaths. Concentrate on sounding precise. Don't allow him to see you as weak.*

"You don't sound fine. Is anyone else in your house with you, or do you have any neighbors you can call? Are you having an episode like before?"

His questions remain unanswered. The phone, which was slapping against my ear due to my trembling hand, now lies on the covers beside me. I inform my arms of their need to move and press against the mattress so that I can lift myself to a standing position, but they refuse to rise, remaining completely inert. Paralysis overtakes my limbs. My eyes dart around the room for signs of someone, something, anything to help, as claustrophobia swarms my senses.

*Keep breathing, Cindy, keep breathing.*

The voice on the phone continues speaking to me, only inches away from my motionless head.

"Cindy, I know you can't speak. Jody told me where you live, so I'm getting into my car to come to you. Don't try to move, don't try to speak. Just keep breathing and stay calm. You're going to be all right. Listen to my voice, Cindy. I'm coming to you. Stay with me, Cindy. I'll be right there. Hang on!"

The line clicks dead, and I am left in the void.

I hear the sound of my own breathing, which is more of a constricted gasp than a full breath. Terror floods my thoughts, taunting me like shadows shifting on the ceiling.

*Keep breathing, Cindy, keep breathing. You can't stop breathing.*

In less than three minutes, I hear the front double doors opening.

*Relax, Cindy, he's coming. Jody must have told him about the spare key in the front flower bed. Don't be alarmed; it's not an intruder. It's him.*

Frantic footsteps race up the stairs, arriving outside the bedroom door. The knob turns, but the door remains closed. I hear the pressure of his body leaning heavily against the door, but the double locks hold it securely shut.

"I'm here, Cindy!" his frantic voice yells. "I'm going to find something to break open the door."

His footsteps scamper downstairs and then return a minute later. A blunt object strikes the door, causing it to groan with an aching thud. The object returns for a second blow. This time the sound of wood splintering resonates from the door. A third impact rattles with a metallic burst as the double locks become dislodged from their slot in the wall. With a final surge, the object sends the wooden barrier flinging open.

Tony appears in the doorway. His face is covered with sweat and his eyes are bulging with fear-fueled courage. He steps into the room and tosses aside a bulky remnant of one of the ancient center room statues. Then he moves to the side of the bed, reaches beneath my torso and legs, and lifts me into the air. My eyes stare at him, transfixed and traumatized.

"It's okay, I'm here," he speaks with startling composure.

He carries me out of the bedroom and we travel down the length of the staircase to arrive at the center room. He quickens his pace and leads us through the open front doorway to his waiting car in the circle drive. After laying me down on the already leaned back passenger seat, he races back to close and lock the front doors. Then he hustles to the car, closes the passenger door, and circles the vehicle to slide into the driver's seat.

"Hang on, Cindy. Stay with me." His offbeat voice is strangely calming.

As the vehicle moves around the circle drive and winds along the gravel path to the main road, he keeps his left hand on the steering wheel and places his right hand on my forehead. His touch is like fire, even though I flush with embarrassment at him having to feel my clammy forehead smeared with sweat.

"I'm right here, Cindy. I'm taking you to the hospital. Don't worry, we'll be there soon."

He looks at me with eyes of understanding. Then he removes his hand from my forehead and lowers it to my left hand.

"I'm here," he reiterates, squeezing my hand fiercely.

I can sense the pressure of his grip and it strikes me as unnerving how comforting his touch feels. My eyes watch his feverish face as he alternates between staring ahead at the road and glancing over to make sure I am still lying beside him.

As we travel for the next several minutes, it seems he cannot find the right words, any words, to assure me. The singular task of whisking me away to safety consumes him; it is etched on his strained face. The casual, carefree comedian has disappeared, leaving a frightened, tortured man in his place. His silence, however, is not the main cause of my alarm; instead, it is the feeling of cherished connection in the simple act of his holding my hand that looms more haunting to me than my paralysis. I worry that when we reach the hospital, he will let go of me, but I find myself conflicted because I wish he would release me at once so I will not have to rely on him for support or strength. We journey in pleasantly painful silence until arriving at the hospital entrance, while his grasp around my hand only increases in intensity with each passing minute.

# *Chapter Eight*

My eyelids open slowly, allowing the burn of blinding light to barrage my overly sensitive eyes. The ceiling appears blurry, the white, corrugated panels looming in my vision like snow-covered squares. After a few blinks, I become aware that I am lying on a hospital bed.

I hear three voices chatting with animated conversation. I instantly recognize Jody's and Samantha's voices, but who is the third person? The voice is far too deep to be a woman's voice.

"She's awake!" Jody exclaims from somewhere below my feet. "Samantha, let's go get the doctor."

I listen to their scampering feet click—click—click on the tile floor. Only a moment passes before Tony's face is hovering over my head, looking down at me with a knowing smile.

"I missed you," he says, searching my eyes.

My eyes repeat the sentiment to him. "Thank—you—" I speak with painful slowness. The connection between my thoughts and my mouth feels tenuous.

"You've been asleep for almost an hour," he says, his increasingly handsome face only inches away from mine.

"Am I—okay?"

"*I* think so. But they have people running around in white jackets who need to take a look at you to determine for themselves. You're not going back to work for a while, that's for certain."

I feel the protest rising in me. "But—"

"Don't even think about it, Cindy. I haven't known you for long, but I know you're a workaholic and a wonderfully uptight one at that. Work will only agitate whatever is being activated by stress. You need progressive therapy, period."

He sees my eyes grow large with fear. "Please don't—make me go," I whisper, my voice so timid and wispy that I wonder if I even spoke the words aloud.

"Relax," he says, placing a hand on my shoulder. "I'm not going to send you to some random shrink to pick you apart and medicate you into oblivion. I have a very special brand of therapy in mind."

Footsteps sound from the doorway. Dr. Shipper enters the room with his authoritative, upright posture. Samantha and Jody trail in behind him, beaming at the sight of me fully conscious.

"Hi, Dr. Shipper," I say weakly.

"Well, Ms. James, once again, you have manifested symptoms of health conditions that you do not have, according to the additional tests we've run tonight. I have no doubt that you are suffering from a stress disorder, with deeper underlying issues causing the stress to trigger these episodes. I have consulted with Mr. Prost, and we have come up with a course of therapy which we believe will be more beneficial than mere stress management. There must be some unremembered, unvisited trauma in your mind that wants to force its way out. It is using your body as the tool for its expression. Unfortunately, besides a standard dose of a serotonin inhibitor which will help balance your chemical levels and enable you to process stress better, there is nothing else we can do for you at this point. I urge you to take care of yourself. You must understand how vital your responsibility is in your own recovery. I strongly advise you to take an indefinite leave of absence from work until both the serotonin inhibitor and the course of therapy I've prescribed have had time to garner some demonstrated progress for you. Will this be acceptable to you?"

My eyes glance from his face over to Tony's. My therapist nods.

"Yes, doctor," I reply candidly.

"Very good. Now, you may rest here as long as you need. Once you are ready to head home, the nurse will bring you your discharge paperwork and you are free to be driven home. Have a good evening, Ms. James."

He smiles and reaches across the bed to shake Tony's hand.

"Good to see you again, Tony."

Tony grins. "You too, John. Take it easy."

They release their grip and Dr. Shipper exits swiftly. Samantha and Jody race to the side of the bed, unable to contain their anxiousness.

"Do you really think she can get well?" Samantha asks.

All eyes move to Tony. He shrugs. "That's up to Cindy here."

All eyes move to me. I glance away and smile awkwardly. "So it seems you all are friends now?"

Jody nods decisively and gestures toward Tony. "Anyone who saves my best friend is a friend of mine."

I close my eyes for a moment, trying to compose my nerves. In the darkness of my shut eyes, the image of a wrinkled picture of Mama and me nags at my memory. The pink color of the wall in the background of the picture has disappeared, being replaced by a rich red. Yet I cannot remember why the wall—why all the walls—turned red. In the silent blankness of my closed eyes, I am not able to see the reason, so it must be something forgotten, which means it must have never happened.

*** 

The sleepless air suspended throughout the house waits outside of the closed kitchen door. Safely insulated on the other side of the industrial ovens and cattle trough-sized sinks, Jody and I sit with our legs dangling over the edge of the ten-foot wide stainless steel countertop. Half eaten sandwiches oozing with smoked turkey and provolone cheese—a late night Achilles heal for me—lay surrounded by crumbs on top of paper plates. The last hour has passed with idle conversation.

"Is it something I said?" I hear Jody ask me.

Snapping back to awareness, I focus on her face and smile with embarrassment.

"Sorry, I was daydreaming."

She grins. "Well, it's one in the morning, so I believe that's considered night dreaming. It's been a while since we've done this."

"Way too long," I reply, sensing memories tugging me away once more.

Jody fidgets restlessly.  "How are you *really* feeling? And none of this 'I'm fine, I'm totally fine' nonsense.  Give me the truth."

My eyes swerve away from her toward the stove top. "Sometimes the weakness— the heaviness in my limbs and the tremoring—overpowers me.  I feel prone to episodes at any time, no matter how much I rest and no matter how much I try to reduce my stress.  When I want to sleep, I can't, and when I want to stay awake because I'm worried and anxious, my body sleeps without warning or it shuts down and I can't move.  It's terrifying.  I feel like I have no control over myself."

"That's screwed up," Jody marvels.  "You've been out of the hospital for a week already.  I thought surely your body would have leveled out by now."

I look at her with panic in my eyes.  Regret is already gnawing at my insides, but desperation overrides reasoning.

"I need you to give me something to help me, Jody. Something to numb the pain, to settle the anxiety, to stifle the tremors.  The stuff the doctor gave me is not enough.  Surely you have some samples from work with you.  I'm not asking for a lot of them, just a few I can try to find one that works."

"But, Cindy—"

"Jody, I *need* them.  It's not unethical for me to ask for samples.  Whatever you can scrounge together will be fine. Only enough to knock me out for a while or to calm things down when I'm awake.  Don't you have anything with you?"

She sighs and reaches over to her purse.  After rifling through the contents for a few moments, she pulls out a few packets with drug company logos on them.  Her eyes delve into mine with sobering focus.

"I had a feeling you'd be asking me for something soon. Try any one of these when you're feeling over the edge and it should bring you back down."

She places them into my grasping hand.  I receive the pilfered prizes with reverence and place them securely into my pocket.

"How did you get them?  Like usual?"

"Yep," she answers, glancing away.  "Extras from the supply room.  We're allowed to take them.  Just never thought I'd be running stuff out of the pharmacy for anyone other than me."

"Feeling guilty?" I ask, offering a supportive smile.

She shrugs. "Not guilty. Just cautious. I don't want to screw you up more than you already are."

"Thanks for that," I reply, smacking her thigh with my open palm.

She smiles wryly. "Always glad to help. Just don't abuse them and make me end up hurting you with them. I threw in a couple sleep-aids as well, just in case."

"Can't wait," I say, grinning.

"Be careful with that crap. I don't want you overdosing or taking a cocktail of multiple samples all at the same time. That'll mess with your head, and you'll end up slitting your wrists or something."

She perceives the frozen look in my eyes.

"Sorry, Cindy, I didn't mean it. That was thoughtless."

I smile to break the tension. "No worries. Honest mistake. I'll be careful."

An unnerving pause distances us for a moment, but Jody dispels it by slipping off the countertop and onto her feet.

"I'll check in on you tomorrow night. Is Tony coming during the day?"

"Yes, he's going to start his new run-my-life therapy marathon. I'm not looking forward to it. I've had such a rocky relationship with him so far. I don't know how his trying to fix me will improve things for us."

Jody leans across the countertop to grab her purse. "Give him time, Cindy. I'm sure he's just like those sample pills. If it doesn't work at first, keep trying and you'll find your fix eventually. Now take some pharmacy magic, go to bed, and get some sleep."

I slide off the countertop and land on my feet a bit unsteadily. We hug and then she lets me go, making sure to shoot me a warning stare.

"That stuff is to help you get rested, not reckless, okay?"

I nod and look away while she moves to the door on the opposite side of the kitchen. My feet slowly follow her, as I place my hand near the samples in my pocket, feeling the smallness of their shape yet sensing the heaviness of their presence. Upon reaching the center room, I gaze out into the dark interior of the house, realizing it will be a long, disturbing night, pills or no pills.

# *Chapter Nine*

My eyes focus on Tony's face, which has the ridiculous coincidence of glowing amid the afternoon rays of sun peeking in through the far library window. His sunlit skin appears radiant, but this is clearly not what I should be thinking about him. Warm mugs of steaming coffee rest on the end tables beside each of the comfortable armchairs.

Tony sits close to the window, while I am safely positioned by the desk. During the first ten minutes since he arrived, we have shared a total of six lines of dialogue about my general health. He was inquisitive; I was guarded. Typical. The last three minutes have consisted of aimless eye wanderings for both of us. At this agonizing rate, I might actually wish for the night to come quickly.

"I don't get it," Tony begins, circling his eyes back to mine.

"Don't get what?" I ask, trying to act aloof.

"This house—this gigantic, barren place—and you living here all alone. I hope you have a maid?"

"No, I do it all myself."

He starts to smile but then withdraws, unsure whether to marvel at my statement or scoff at the ludicrous logistics involved. "I don't think I would have pegged you for the domestic type, no offense."

A smile forms on my mouth. "None taken. So, how did you peg me?"

He folds his arms, pretends to be sizing me up, and raises an eyebrow. "The driven, career woman type. Workaholic, no time for relationships, got-it-all-together girl. The same categorical stereotype I'm not supposed to squeeze you into."

I bite my lower lip. "You'd be right."

He grows intrigued. His hand, which had been stretching for his coffee, leaves the mug untouched and leans forward with the rest of him in his chair. "I was right in my assessment of you?"

"No, you were right that you shouldn't try to squeeze me into your stereotype box. I may be more and I may be less than your box, but I certainly won't fit myself in there."

"Fair enough," he replies, resting his elbows on his knees and interlocking his fingers in a contemplative posture. "No more labels. But I'm burning to know, what's with this house? When I dashed in here the other night, there were candles lit in every room. The walls were creaking and groaning. There are massive shadows everywhere. How do you sleep here?"

My eyes search the floor for safety. "You get used to it. I don't think of it as abnormal anymore."

He allows the words to sink in for a moment. His eyes reach out to pull mine back to his face, but I offer my strongest resistance. "How long have you lived here?"

I sigh and let my eyes be drawn to his. "Probably all of my life. I can't remember anything before this place."

After leaning back in the armchair, he lifts his right leg and crosses it over his left knee. "Have you ever wanted to move? I'm sure this place is a burden to maintain."

"I don't ever allow myself to think about it," I reply hastily. "It's my house, it's where I live, and this is what was left to me."

He releases my eyes and looks away to the desk beside me. "So, the candles in the rooms each night, is that for aesthetics or safety?"

He tries to put me at ease with a laid back grin, but I refuse to take the bait.

"You wouldn't understand. And don't say, 'try me,' as if you actually could. It's just what I choose to do and I'm not asking you to understand it."

His eyes dart back to mine, appearing amused. "Sorry, didn't know it was a sore spot. I was only asking because surely you are aware what a fire hazard burning candles next to window curtains can be."

I feel my face turning crimson. "I'm aware of the risk." My voice is cold.

"Good, so am I ever going to get a tour of this place? What on earth do you fill so many rooms in a house with?"

I sense my eyes closing momentarily, being whisked away to memories threatening to flash across my mind.  The pull of remembrance rises like a pale-faced specter, revealing images chilling enough to haunt me all the way into the abyss.  Then I force my eyes open and see him gazing at me, mystified.  My mouth opens and speaks with wavering thinness.

"The rooms used to be filled with things.  Each room had furniture, pictures, fine linens, and memories.  Then they were removed.  Now the only room with anything in it, besides these rooms downstairs, is my bedroom."

Tony stares at me intently—causing the nerves to flutter within me.  He sits in contented silence, no smile, no wink, no childish grin.  Just the quietude of his perceiving that he has gained some new understanding of me.

"Why?" he asks at last.

I stare at the floor, sensing the ghosts whispering, lurking, clawing, ready to pull me six feet under to face their grave truths.  "As I said, you wouldn't understand."  I hear the impatience in my voice.

He stares at me, his silence allowing the dread to stalk my thoughts feverishly.

*Remember, Cindy. All you have to do is remember. The memories are waiting. They're waiting for you.*

*No, I don't want to remember, Cindy. Once the first image comes, they won't stop coming. This is the one that starts it all. It's the first memory I recall, but the last one I want to relive.*

*Let me remind you. Let me help you return to when it all began.*

*Please, let me keep forgetting. I've resisted you for longer than I even know. You've been buried, gone.*

*Yes, that's why it's time to come back. It's time to come home. I'm waiting.*

*Leave me alone! I don't want to go back.*

*Sweet, stupid Cindy. I've finally found you, and I'm never going away.*

I shift uneasily in my chair, closing and opening my eyes several times.  "So what's this new therapy you're going to try on me?" I ask, offering my best aloof tone.

"What do you think we've been doing?" he says candidly. His trademark grin returns. "Cindy, you know as well as I do that I'm totally incapable of fixing you. The only solution for you is to perform therapy on yourself and simply use me as a sounding board. You're going to talk yourself to health. I believe this house is the secret to uncovering whatever is buried within you. That's why we're here. So if you want the health episodes to stop, I suggest you start talking the hell out of yourself. I'm going to the kitchen to make sandwiches for us. When I get back, you better be ready to talk to me. I'll see you in five minutes."

Without another word, he rises from his chair and leaves the room. I sit in silence, sensing a throbbing pain pressing against my temples, as a single mental image flashes in my mind. I press my palms against my forehead to squelch the rising tumult, while I see the young girl beneath her bed, covering her ears and hiding in terror.

*Yes, that's it, Cindy. Let yourself remember.*

*Push it away, Cindy. Don't be swallowed by it. Resist the pull.*

*Don't listen to her. You must remember. You must come back.*

*Look away from the girl. Remembering her will destroy you.*

*Please, let me run to her.*

*Please, let me run away from her.*

The young girl feels close enough to touch.

*Reach out to her. Speak to her. Free her. Open your eyes.*

*Save yourself. Forget her. Close your eyes! Close your eyes!*

Suddenly, I open my eyes to find the underside of my bed. My hands are covering my ears and my tears are running thickly onto the floor to splash against the backs of the cockroaches scurrying below me. Headless Raggedy Ann lies pinned between my elbows and my stomach. The muffled sound of a heavy object striking the kitchen wall slithers into my ears past the tiny slits between my trembling fingers. I begin humming Mama's song.

"*Rain, rain, go away, come again another day. Rain, rain, go away, come again another day.*"

As I wait for the horrible noises from the kitchen to stop, my mind wanders to the conversation Mama and I had last night. "It's the mothers who keep the whole show running," she said. "It's the mothers who have nothing better to do," Daddy yelled from the couch. I looked at Mama with a smile, letting her know I agreed with her.

Puberty injected its lethal dose into my body this year, and now I wish I didn't want to like boys. It's difficult at school because I'm not a tomboy or a tiara-wearing princess, but simply a color-within-those-lines girl stuck in a family drowning in poverty. No boy will ever like me, I'm sure of it. He'll be able to tell all my clothes are from the Goodwill. He'll know my daddy's a wife beater. He'll see the outside of our shack of a house and never darken the door of my life with a family like this waiting inside.

My teacher says I have been too self-consciousness in class for a bright thirteen-year-old girl; she says I should be proud of myself. I don't see what my teacher thinks she can see in me, because I only see myself as worthy of shame, and I wish Mama knew how to convince me that feeling this way could be something other than normal.

No scream echoes throughout the house, but I hear Mama's body smacking against the kitchen wall again. My mind goes back to yesterday. I remember wondering how Daddy could be an abuser when he didn't drink and he didn't use drugs. Surely he'd have to be using something to alter his senses in order to wail on Mama, but I guess, just like my shame, I have to accept it as something normal.

Daddy fights with his fists and Mama fights with her silence. A few minutes from now, it will all be over. Daddy will kick the front door open and roar off in his truck. Mama will wash her face and arms with a washcloth and let me know when it's safe to come out to see her.

Daddy will be gone until I'm supposed to be asleep tonight. Tomorrow, he'll traipse off to work at the lumber yard as if nothing happened. It's always in the nighttime that I'm glad no one lives within half a mile of us, or else they would see the ruckus, but it's always in the daytime that I wish we lived closer to someone, so they could see the ruckus and help us.

A door slams from across the house. I remove my hands from my ears and wait. After a few minutes, I hear the kitchen faucet finally turn off.

"You can come out, baby," Mama's voice calls wearily.

I crawl out from under the bed, place Raggedy Ann on my pillow, pry open my creaking bedroom door, and walk down the hallway to the kitchen. Mama sits at the far end of the wobbly kitchen table. Two bowls of late night snack cereal are already prepared. I take my seat next to her and we stare at each other in silence. I try to stay strong, not wanting to add to her tears by spilling any of my own. The new bruises on her face are already blending in with the old bruises. Her face color always seems to be a constant mix of peach and purple. Makeup can only hide so much blood pooling to the cheeks in her face; she'll have to apply some extra layers of concealer for work tomorrow. We sit at the table, uninterested in the generic brand corn flakes bought with food stamps. Our mouths never move, but our eyes continue communicating our mutual desperation, adding wrinkles to the secret plan we've been making for the past four years since the beatings began. The way she looks at me tonight tells me tomorrow is the time to make our escape. I close my eyes, wishing we could vanish together to somewhere safe.

When I open my eyes, it's already tomorrow, Tuesday, a hot and muggy day in May of 1973. The bell has just rung at noon to dismiss class. It's the final day of the school year. I make my way toward the cafeteria along with my classmates, but I take a short cut through the library and dart across the hallway by the gym to the outer door leading to the back parking lot. As planned, Mama has already taken off her McDonald's apron for the last time after completing her shift at the hash brown deep fryer this morning. She's gone home, packed up as many things as she can fit into a garbage bag, and then walked the two miles to school.

As I sneak out through the back door of the gym, I find Mama leaning her heavy frame against the side of the building, breathing hoarsely, her pasty white skin slick with sweat. The bulky garbage bag rests at her feet.

"Time to go, baby," she says, reaching down to retrieve the bag. I have my school backpack strapped around my shoulders. We look around to make sure no one is watching and then we head in the opposite direction from the main road, cutting through a patch of woods.

Between the trees I can spot Lookout Mountain in the distance, the only place I can go in Chattanooga where no one can find me. Sometimes, I escape there after school. Mama knows the two-mile walk from school back home should only take me an hour or so, but she must know I have visited Lookout Mountain on days when it takes me two or three hours to get home, because she never scolds me and never asks me where I was. She has enough to think about with Daddy getting home later that night.

"Where are we going, Mama?"

Her face remains focused ahead, her eyes intense with something resembling wildness. "Away from your daddy, baby. Away from your daddy."

We walk a mile before coming to the bus stop. We wait only a few minutes before the bus swings around the corner and pulls up to the curbside. The exhaust whips into my face, making me nauseous. Mama and I move toward the bus anxiously, while several people in front of us clamber up the bus stairs.

Then we hear a familiar rattling sound behind us. I turn around and see Daddy's beat up red Ford truck coming to a stop. Daddy sits in the driver's seat with hatred in his eyes.

"Get in here!" his voice bellows.

I start walking to the truck out of shut-mouthed habit, but Mama grabs my arm and pulls me back toward the bus.

"Don't get on that bus!" Daddy yells. "If you get on that bus, I'll come after you. Lisa, don't make me come after you. Don't make me come after Cindy. You know I will."

I glance around, hoping someone will notice, someone will help, but everyone looks down and quickly climbs into the safety of the bus as if nothing is happening outside.

Suddenly, Mama releases my arm and turns back to the truck. "Get in the truck, baby."

I start to tremble, looking up at her. "Why, Mama?"

"Because we're going home," she says sternly. I notice tears in her eyes.

We make our way slowly over to Daddy's truck and climb inside—after Mama puts the garbage bag in the flatbed. I get into the truck first, making sure to sit between them so that Daddy will have a farther reach to hit Mama. He has never touched me, so I know I will be safe, but Mama will surely be pummeled tonight, so I want to spare her some hits during the drive home.

"Filthy woman," Daddy says to Mama, as spit squirts out between his clenched teeth. "The one day I drive home to have lunch, and you're trying to take my daughter away from me. If we weren't in broad daylight, I'd beat you 'til your eyes were swollen shut.

Don't you *ever* try to leave me again.  You don't want our darling Cindy here to be without a Mama, do you?"

The bus has already pulled away and disappeared around the corner on its way to freedom.  Daddy revs the coughing engine and we head toward home in tense silence.  As we ride, I bite my lower lip and think about Mama.  I wish I could grab her hand and take her to Lookout Mountain with me.  The evening performance the stars put on when you are standing at the edge of one of the campfire pits near the rock cleft is breathtaking.  If only Mama could see it, then she could have hope for something different.  Maybe one day.

The truck sputters hoarsely as we pull up to stop in the dirt driveway.  Mama and I get out of the truck and hurry inside.  Daddy stays in the truck for a minute.

"Go to your room, baby.  Cover your ears, and don't come out, no matter what happens," Mama says to me.

I look her in the face, hoping in some small way to comfort her from what we both know is about to happen.  Her eyes are sad, but not despairing.  I see the same wildness in her eyes that I had seen earlier today.  Her eyes let me know that she will be all right, that we will somehow be all right.  I give her a quick hug and then race to my room, hearing the floor creaking under me as I hide beneath my bed.

Moments later, I hear the front door shut roughly.  Mama's body slams against the kitchen wall.

Then I hear a different sound, the sound of a scream.  But it isn't Mama's voice.  The scream is followed by moaning sounds.

I crawl out from underneath my bed and creep over to my bedroom door.  After inching open the door, I peek out into the hallway.  I can't get a good angle of sight into the kitchen, so I quietly step into the hallway.  The moaning sound from Daddy continues drifting eerily into my ears.  I pause for a moment, waiting.  Then I slowly make my way into the kitchen.

I see Mama standing over Daddy, gripping a large kitchen knife in her hand, the same knife she uses to carve the turkey that those ladies from the church downtown bring us each Thanksgiving.  The knife has blood smeared across it.  The look of wildness is still raging in her eyes.  She uses the back of her hand to wipe dribbling blood away from her nose.

I am so shocked that it takes me a few seconds to look down at Daddy. I feel a mixture of relief, nausea, and horror filling my stomach as I stare at him. A gaping, bloody wound is spread across the place on his chest where his heart should be. His eyes are open and his breathing is labored, while the blood running down his shirt starts pooling on the floor. He is still alive, but I'm not sure how much longer that will be the case.

Mama turns to look at me. The wildness in her expression turns to anguish when she sees me. She drops the knife, which clangs against the dirty tile. The sound of the metal blade crashing against the floor storms into my ears like thunder. With her eyes still fastened to mine, she rubs her hands against her pants to dry off the blood.

"It's time to go, baby," she says, almost in a whisper. "Go to your room and pack everything you can into your backpack. Be quick about it. Understood?"

"Yes, Mama."

I turn and head back to my room, rummaging through my belongings and stuffing everything I can fit into my backpack, making sure to leave room for Raggedy Ann. I hear Daddy's muffled moaning. I try to ignore the sound as I look around in a daze at my tattered Barbie bedspread and my hand-me-down Easy Bake oven set. My eyes stare at the far wall, picturing Daddy's bleeding chest.

After a minute, Mama's heavy footsteps lumber across the kitchen.

"Let's go, baby."

I grab my backpack, stand up, say good-bye to my room, and walk out.

When I return to the kitchen, Daddy is still lying in his own blood, his eyes glazed like the icing on a donut. Sweat pours down his face like running water from a faucet. He is having trouble breathing, the noise from his throat sounding as raspy as the truck engine getting started.

"Cindy," he croaks. "Don't leave me. You help your daddy."

Tears fill my eyes and my hands start shaking. "Mama," my voice squeaks, "I'm scared."

"Let's go, baby," Mama repeats, grabbing my hand and dragging me to the door.

Daddy's pale, bloody hand reaches for me, swiping at my leg. "You get—back here—you filthy—"

"Mama!" I scream, cowering away from his grasp.

Mama yanks my arm, nearly ripping it out of its socket. "Come on, baby, we gotta go!" Her voice is frantic, her face deathly white. I almost tumble out into the yard, but her painful grip on my arm keeps me steady. With her free hand, she slams the door shut behind us.

As we bolt for the beat up truck, I hear Daddy stirring in the kitchen. He is banging around, trying to stand and make his way to the door.

"Get in the truck!" Mama yells, flinging open the door.

I climb in as quickly as I can, feeling her roughly push me from behind. Just as Mama scoots in beside me, the front door bursts open. Daddy's horrible figure stands in the doorway, shuddering with shock and oozing blood. His eyes are burning, trying to focus on our faces.

"Don't make me—come after you! I'll—kill you!"

He staggers onto the front grass as Mama starts the coughing engine to life.

"Go, Mama! He's coming!" my voice rings like the school bell.

She shifts the lever on the side of the steering wheel, mashes her foot to the floor, and launches the truck forward, nearly mowing Daddy over as he raises his fists to fight. This time, his fists can't hurt Mama. The truck swings onto the street and drives us away from the bleeding, cursing man and the only house I've ever known.

We race down the highway for several minutes before I sense myself breathing again. I look over at her with wide, watery eyes.

"Will we see Daddy anymore?"

Her voice is low, almost scary in how steady it is. "He's gone, out of our lives. He's not coming back, and we're not going back."

"Doesn't he know where to find us?"

"No, baby. He doesn't know where we're going. Nobody in our family knows where we're going."

It is deadly silent for a long time. I look out at the road and then look back at her.

"So where are we going, Mama?"

"To a new home."

"Where's that?"

"Wherever we are," she answers, keeping her eyes straight ahead.

I can't think of the right words to respond, so I say nothing. I watch Mama for another minute, waiting for her to reach over and hold my shaking hand and explain what just happened. But she simply stares forward without flinching. The image of Daddy standing in the doorway, covered in blood, threatening to kill us, continues flashing in my mind. Closing my eyes tightly, I feel like there is a fight inside of me between two people, a fight that scares me to death.

*Forget what just happened, Cindy. Just forget all about it. It wasn't real. It didn't happen. Say it to yourself, "I don't remember." Say it.*

*No, Cindy, of course it happened. Daddy hates me. He wanted to kill me. I can't forget that. I need to remember it.*

*Just pretend it's disappearing, like a magic trick. The curtain falls over Daddy, who's bloody and cursing and saying he'll kill you, and then—wait for it—wait for it—abracadabra—lift the curtain—and he's gone!*

*It doesn't work that way, Cindy. If you want to keep your head on straight, you'll always remember it. You have to repeat it in your mind so you'll be careful.*

*You're a sweet, stupid girl, Cindy. You need to hide it, like a dead stray cat. Just bury it and no one will know—not even you will know after a while. Say it, "I don't remember."*

*No, I want to remember and never forget!*

*Shut up, Cindy! Now you do as I say or you'll get us both in trouble. Mama will hate you because you made us move away. She'll come after you too unless you push this out of your mind and never bring it up again.*

*I—don't—want—to—*

*Stop crying, you big baby. Wipe up those tears. You've got to be strong for Mama, strong for us. And the only way to do that is to push the memory down and throw dirt on it. Bury it for both of us.*

*You promise we'll be safe if I forget what happened?*

*Yes, I promise. Now would you quit being so weak and say it with me already. "I don't remember." Say it!*

*I don't remember.*

*That's it, Cindy. I don't remember.*

*I don't remember. I don't remember. I don't remember.*

I open my eyes to see Tony arriving back in the library, holding two plates, each piled with a sandwich and chips. The vividness of the memory is spilling onto my face. His eyes grow large, startled by my pained expression.

"I remember," I say, barely above a whisper. "I need to tell you what happened."

He extends a plate to my outreached hands and quickly takes his seat across from me.

"Let's have it," he says, placing the plate on the end table, immediately forgetting about his food.

# *Chapter Ten*

"Hi, Jody, this is Tony. I know you were supposed to check on Cindy tonight, but our therapy session is going a lot longer than expected, so you don't need to swing by. I'll probably be here most of the night at this rate, so I can make sure she's all right before she goes to bed. Thanks. Have a good night."

Tony places the phone receiver onto the base on the end table beside the empty coffee mug and the plate littered with sandwich and potato chip crumbs. His eyes are intensely focused on my face, awaiting newfound revelations.

"So you never had a memory of yourself of the time before you were thirteen years old until today?"

I fidget with my hands and avoid eye contact. "No, Mama and I didn't speak about it, and I couldn't remember anything before we lived here."

He marvels. "Do you remember you father?"

"Until today I only had a vague, mental image of him as a bitter, distant man, but I had assumed he must have died within the first few years of my life. I had forgotten that I actually knew him. The day we left was the last time I saw him."

"Do you think your father died from the stab wound?"

I glance at him reluctantly. "I don't know. He might have lived or he might have bled to death, but I was too scared to find out later. I didn't want anything to do with him."

Tony drums on his kneecaps with his fingers, as if plotting his next chess move. "He didn't know where you and your mom were going?"

"No."

"How do you know?"

"That's what Mama said."

"So how did you end up here in this house?"

The pulsing sensation in my temples begins erupting again. He observes the change in my demeanor. I grip the sides of my head with my hands, applying as much pressure as possible, desperate to escape what I realize is coming.

"Let yourself go there, Cindy," his voice speaks distantly. My eyes close painfully.

My eyes open peacefully. I stretch my arms, yawn, sit up in the passenger's seat of the truck, and look over at Mama. Her grip on the steering wheel is as tight as when she would vice-grip a cantaloupe before hacking it up with the kitchen knife. Her face is even paler than her usual ghostly-looking flesh color. With her eyes fastened on the highway ahead, she is humming to herself, "*Rain, rain, go away, come again another day.*" Her black hair straggles down in distraught curls, caked with sweat. I can see spots of dried blood at the base of her nostrils. Her pretty face, tightened with a stressful expression, doesn't seem to remember how pretty it is.

"You okay, Mama?"

Her eyes dart over to me, and she forces a smile to grace the edge of her mouth. Then her eyes move back to the road. "I'm all right, baby. You slept for a long time, almost the whole day. Are you feeling better?"

"Yeah, I'm okay. Are you sad, Mama?"

"Not sad, baby. Just ready."

I lean forward, trying to get a better focus on her eyes. "What are you ready for?"

"A different life. Do you understand?"

"Yes, Mama, I understand."

"We're going to see your grandma. No one in our family knows where she lives but me."

"What's she like?"

Mama breathes in a deep sigh and exhales shakily. "She's like us, baby. Strong. She's strong like us. You'll just need to be careful. We'll be safe with her, but be on your guard with her. That's all I can tell you. Now get ready."

She stares ahead, shutting me out while she reenters a silent, private conversation she's been having with herself.

Daddy's rusty red Ford truck turns onto a winding driveway that leads us for at least a full minute back into a dense patch of woods, far away from neighboring houses. My legs are curled up so that my head rests on my knees. I take in the beautiful view—the branches greeting us with rich green leaves and the blooming flowers planted in massive stone pots on either side of the gravel path. I have certainly never been anywhere like this before.

I glance over to see Mama's eyes are fixed on the enormous housing coming into view. She seems not to be surprised by the sights taking my breath away. I gasp at the marvelous marble water fountain in the center of a circle driveway leading up to the double doors of the mansion entrance. The water of the fountain bubbles up and sprays freely in dazzling spirals. A lush garden, plump with tomatoes, zucchini, and other brightly colored treats, sits to the right of the house. A lovely gazebo lies beyond the garden, offset by several wrought iron archways through which visitors can stroll along the expansive flower garden display. A tool shed rests behind the gazebo, probably housing gardening tools. Flowers of zesty purple, deep sea blue, beaming yellow, and pumpkin orange are spread across the grassy area. The scents of these flowers filter into my nostrils as we arrive at the circle drive and swerve around the fountain that whirls wildly with water. A classy white Cadillac is parked on an expansive patch of grass, which appears to be a makeshift parking lot for vehicles to the right of the circle drive. The estate sits surrounded by woods, with a grassy area close to the length of a football field stretching behind the house.

The house itself immediately overwhelms my mind. It has five floors and many rooms on each floor. The outer walls are a cream color, appearing to be freshly painted, although the house seems ancient. Two giant pillars guard the doorway, daring people to pass between them.

Mama puts the truck in park, turns off the engine, and we sit for a moment. She leans over and kisses my forehead.

"We're home," she says with a sigh.

"Okay," I answer, looking her in the eyes, searching for what she really wants to say instead of what it seems she feels she has to say.

"Let's go meet your grandma," she says, smiling weakly.

She breathes deeply, and then I breathe deeply. She opens her door, and then I open my door. After walking around the truck, she moves to my side and grabs my hand. She gives my fingers a tight squeeze and then leads me up the stone stairs, past the towering pillars, and to the double doors. Before she even knocks, the door sweeps open.

"Please, come in," a gray-haired man wearing a saggy face and a finely pressed suit says, as he pulls the door open.

"Thank you, Harold," Mama says.

We slowly step inside.

"Good to see you again, Ms. James. I will fetch your things from the vehicle and place them in your respective rooms. She was not expecting your arrival for another few minutes, so she expressed her desire for you to look around and make yourselves at home. She will be down shortly."

The old man's tired eyes move from Mama's face to mine. He winks at me and smiles. Then he turns and exits through the doorway.

Mama and I glance at each other, half amused, half astonished. As we step into the spacious entryway, my eyes wander to the five levels of the house's interior stretching up as far as I imagine heaven can reach. The banisters forming the barrier of each hallway have detailed wooden carvings. It appears that two bedrooms and a bathroom sit on the left and right walls within each of the four upper levels, while a single room sits on the far wall, making twenty regular rooms and eight bathrooms total, without even counting the rooms on the first floor. A polished wooden floor rests beneath our feet. Two life-sized stone statues of goddess-looking women clothed in flowing robes stand on either side of a wooden stand supporting a basket sprawling with dozens of gorgeous flowers.

Mama and I cautiously inch further across the main floor, which, as I crane my neck and look straight upward, leads to a gigantic empty space between the levels, a fifty-foot by thirty-foot—I'm guessing—area flooded by sunlight. The rich pocket of light is like an invisible elevator heading right up to where goddesses must live. As I gaze into the bewildering atmosphere, I feel as if I might climb in my mind to the top floor from where I could take in the entire essence of this place.

"Go ahead, take a look around," Mama encourages.

I release her hand and meander to the left, smelling the wonderful scent of lasagna drifting in from the kitchen. After opening a massive wooden door and creeping inside, I find several tall refrigerators and freezers, as well as wide burners and ovens. A single chef dressed in a white apron is busy plating food. The woman chef is a middle-aged lady, slender, and beautiful with tufts of blonde hair peeking out from beneath her chef's hat. The aroma in the room fills my nostrils and makes my stomach rumble. Before the chef can notice me, I turn and open the large wooden door to escape back into the center room.

Mama is standing still, as if stuck in some memory. Her eyes have a numbed stare. She hardly seems to notice me coming back toward her. I don't want to disturb her, so I wander in the direction straight ahead of where she is standing. Within moments, my feet carry me into a cathedral-like dining room. The walls of white have various paintings of countrysides. A table as long as eight of Daddy's trucks stretches out from one side of the room to the other. There must be forty chairs set behind expensive looking china dishes surrounded by forks, spoons, and knives. Sparkling wine glasses placed at the upper right corner of each plate have shapely napkins tucked neatly into them. The table centerpieces are wreaths decorated with summer flowers, which are wrapped around bowl lamps containing white candles. Maybe the President himself will be eating here tonight.

Backtracking into the center room, I find Mama continuing her stare into nothing. I'm beginning to worry about her. After taking a step toward her, I decide to leave her alone for another minute. I must know what else waits for me in this house.

I dart to the left and open a set of wooden double doors. Once inside, I feel the same giddy sensation I had after seeing that boy in gym class looking at me and smiling a month ago. Towering bookcases line the walls of the room, filled with thousands of books staring back at me. This room seems as large as the library at school. A bathroom door with gold plating stands at the far corner of the room, directly across from a rustic fireplace, and a few feet behind a plush white couch covered with a green afghan. A desk of dark wood sits in the right corner near a large end table, covered with a lamp and some pictures. In the left corner, a comfortable reading chair and an end table rest beside a window. The sunshine entering the room through the window warms me inside. I feel light in here, in every room. I'm glad this place is home. I close my eyes and hope I'll always remember how I feel right now.

As I come back to the center room, I see Mama still standing as if in a stupor.

"Are you okay, Mama?" I ask, arriving at her side and grabbing her hand.

"I'm fine, baby. Totally fine," she answers, sounding more unconvinced of it than I am.

Suddenly, an unfamiliar, upbeat voice rings throughout the house. "You've come at last!"

Mama and I look up to observe a woman in a bizarre, glittering white robe, sweeping down the stairs to the bottom floor where we stand. Her bright blonde hair seems more blonde than it should be, like the gray color has been covered up with streaks of fake yellow. Her face should have wrinkles, but it also has an unnatural quality to it, as if it's been flattened with an iron. The bright blue color in her eyes seems alien. Her skin is leathery, like it's been left out too long to bake in the sun. She wears silver multi-hoop earrings that flash with a tint of fiery orange. Her fingers have rings of dazzling stones that reflect the sunlight around the room like bolts of lightning.

I grip Mama's hand even tighter. Mama does not take a step forward, but waits as the mysterious woman seems to float across the floor to us.

"Hi, Mom," says Mama blandly. They embrace briefly and then withdraw.

"Hi, Lisa. You've come back at last. Welcome home," the lady speaks, her voice commanding and penetrating. She bores her eyes into Mama's face, as if trying to read her thoughts. Without warning, her eyes fall on me, their captivating quality inescapable. "So you must be my dear granddaughter, Cindy Jeanetta."

I stare up at her, half terrified and half entranced. No one ever uses my middle name. Mama has only called me with my middle name one time before, the time she caught me trying to force feed dirty silverware to the stray cat living under the house. I remember apologizing for my actions, realizing I should have used clean silverware instead.

"Hi," I hear myself saying shyly in response to the goddess.

I watch her, wide-eyed, as she drifts over and enfolds her elegant arms around me with the gracefulness of a ballet dancer. The nearness of her presence feels somewhat comforting and somewhat disturbing. Who *is* this woman, and how did she come to live here in heaven?

After releasing my inferior body, the angelic figure stretches her hand toward the dining room. "You must be hungry. Our chef, Marlene, should be finishing the meal preparations. I will show you to your rooms soon enough, but first, we must have you eat something. Follow me."

We trail behind the floating someone who is supposedly my grandma. Mama's eyes are glazed, her expression blank. My eyes are darting about wildly, taking in the scene. As we make our way toward the dining room, my hand clenches Mama's hand fiercely. I feel the iciness in her fingers, and I begin wondering what happened between her and this foreign goddess who is leading us further into our new home. I blink, and the house disappears in my mind.

My eyes open and resurface to see Tony eagerly waiting for me. He leans forward in his chair, ready to pounce.

"Where did you go?"

I stare at him. "I came back to this house, for the first time I was here. When I met Grandma."

"What happened? How was she?"

My eyes grow quiet. I slowly rise from the chair and inch toward the open doorway. "I don't know that I'm ready for all of this at once. Remembering is important, but I think I've had enough for one day."

He stands up and folds his arms. "I understand. You need to go at your own pace."

I smile, fatigued. "Thanks."

"Of course. Are you going to be okay for tonight?"

"I'll be fine. I have my pills to help me sleep."

His eyes grow inquisitive. "The pills the doctor gave you, right?"

"Yes—those pills. *Only* those pills, of course." My eyes swerve to the floor.

"I hope you get some good rest. If you feel up to it, can you do me a favor?"

"Sure."

"As you remember things, will you write them down? It should help jog your recollection, and it will help me catch up with your memories."

I nod slowly. "I can do that."

He moves to the open doorway. "Well, I'll let you get some rest. It's been a good day together."

A flutter in my heart quickens. "Yes, it's been a good day."

"We'll catch up sometime next week to see how you're doing, if that's all right with you."

"I'd like that."

An awkward pause settles between us as we make eye contact and then look away from each other. He breaks the tension by heading to the front double doors. Before opening the door, he swivels around and smiles.

"I'm proud of you, Cindy. You're a strong, brave woman. Good night."

I hope the blush in my face is mostly shrouded by the darkness of the center room. "Good night, Tony."

He pulls open the door and slips into the darkness, leaving me standing alone with my swirling thoughts.

# *Chapter Eleven*

The small wick blazes to life, casting flickering shadows across the walls and ceiling. After moving swiftly around the bed, I deposit the long-nosed lighter into the nightstand drawer and step over to double lock the bedroom door, pausing and then turning around with embarrassment at the realization that the door is still broken and dislodged from its hinges due to the force of Tony's emergency entrance several nights ago. I linger by the nightstand and allow the drafty breeze from the house interior to sweep into the room and crawl over my bare feet.

Then I lower my gaze onto the orange, white-capped bottle on the nightstand, labeled with my prescription from Dr. Shipper. I decide to leave the prescription pills undisturbed and grasp instead several different sample packets from Jody, tearing them open and depositing the contents into my palm. I pop various colored pills into my mouth and quickly wash them down with lukewarm water from a glass resting near the alarm clock.

*Find your fix, Cindy. That's it. Kill the pain. Subdue the depression. Just like Mama. Let the medicine soothe you; let it drown the sadness.*

I slink into bed and reach over to retrieve the journal notebook and pen which have been awaiting my arrival. Then I find myself chewing on the pen absent-mindedly, scrounging my mind for a way to begin. With repulsion, I yank the germ-infested object out of my mouth and notice tiny indentions where my teeth were gnawing. I picture Tony and smile. After placing the ink tip on the paper, I watch as the words take shape.

*Mama, I remember the day we were separated. I couldn't bring myself to fully fathom the realization of you stabbing Daddy; I only wanted to think of it as you saving me. Coming to the mansion was supposed to be the new start of something better, and it was a new start, but not of anything we had hoped.*

*I miss you now, and the more I remember, the more it stings, because I know I have to revisit the day I began missing you.*

*The headache is already returning, so I know I will see you soon. I hope this helps me find my way back.*

My eyes open to an empty plate sitting before me, nearly licked clean of lasagna residue. The grandma goddess occupies her head seat at the end of the table. Mama is across from me, her eyes as quiet as her mute voice.

"I hope you enjoyed your lunch, Cindy dear," Grandma says to me, eyeing my plate and then my sauce-stained mouth.

"Yes, thank you," I answer sheepishly.

"Very good, very good," she speaks, as if to herself. "Now, come, I have much to show you. There are many things for you to see in this place." I assume she is speaking to Mama, so I'm already daydreaming about the garden outside. "Cindy dear, are you listening?"

I snap awake, looking into her eyes accidentally. The power of her gaze captivates my imagination.

"Sorry," I mumble.

She smiles, the whiteness of her teeth shining like the headlights on Daddy's truck when he pulls into the driveway late at night. "That's quite all right. Are you interested in seeing what waits for you in this house?"

"I guess so," I reply, glancing over to see Mama's reaction. She remains unresponsive to my eyes.

"Wonderful. I will catch up with your mother soon enough, but you and I have adventures ahead."

The grandma goddess rises from her chair with queenly elegance and claps her hands precisely. Within moments, Harold, the gray-haired butler, enters the room and begins clearing the dishes. He catches me watching him and shoots me a smile and a wink. I smile back and stand up from my seat.

The creature of light sweeps to my side, towering over me with regal authority. "Take my hand. It's time for you to see your new room."

My hand unconsciously slips into her hand, feeling bound as if by an unnatural force. As she leads me out of the dining room, I glimpse Mama's sad, weary expression. Her eyes no longer contain their spark, the fighting quality I witnessed when she was standing over Daddy, holding the carving knife. She makes no effort to raise her eyes to meet mine. Instead, she stares at the table before her blankly, acknowledging nothing and no one.

"This house was built in 1955 by your grandfather," the goddess announces.

"Okay," I answer, feeling my throat catch.

We draw close to the winding staircase at the corner of the center room.

"You can call me Grandma."

"Yes, Grandma."

She smiles supremely and leads me up the stairs to the second level.

"Do you know how long I've been waiting to hear you call me Grandma? Thirteen long years. Since you were born, Cindy dear."

I respond with silence. She stops and leans down to me, the flat-ironed skin of her face betraying no blemishes. A mysterious smile crosses her lips, a smile with a secret hidden in it. "Do you know why we've never met before?"

Her blinding eyes are unavoidable; they pull me in to gaze at her against my will. "I don't know," I hear myself mutter.

Now her voice hushes to a whisper. "Your mother never told you?"

I shake my head robotically. "No, Grandma."

"I've no doubt that she wouldn't. Well, for now, that little tidbit will stay between your mother and me. I'll tell you when you're ready, Cindy dear. Only when you're ready. Understood?"

"Yes, Grandma."

"Now, enough chit chat, we have your new room to visit. Follow me."

She effortlessly ascends the next flight of stairs to the third level, with me clambering obediently at her heels. Upon reaching the top of the stairwell to the intersection of two hallways, she heads down the hallway to the left with her light feet scarcely tiptoeing along the wooden floor. I follow her doggedly, glancing at the polished banister overlooking the massive open space between the levels of the house. My eyes dart back to her, seeing her halt at the single closed door on the wall. The color of the wooden door is a light reddish shade of some beautiful tree. She opens the door and swings it full arch to the doorstop on the other side.

"This way."

She smiles, and then I smile. She moves forward, and then I move forward. I watch her turn and take in my expression as I absorb the sight before me. The walls are bright pink, seeming to sparkle in the sunlight streaming through the window. Frilly curtains of expensive-looking white fabric are draped around the window. A bed lies against the left wall, covered with multiple pink plush pillows and a gorgeous comforter of quilted square patterns outlined in pink. A bookcase filled with books sits in the corner. A wide clothes rack, built right into the wall beside a tall, oval mirror, holds dozens of trendy outfits suspended by hangers. Several pairs of new shoes are positioned at the foot of the bed. My eyes bulge at the sight of all my dreams filling the same room.

"Thank you, Grandma. This is amazing."

"You're welcome, dear. It's all yours. I hope you enjoy it. Now, before we continue with the tour, I'm going to lay out your daily schedule since you are going to live here now."

"Okay," I say hesitantly, wondering if my room is going to be taken away before I even have a chance for it to be mine.

"Your daily schedule will be as follows: Breakfast at 6 a.m.; school lessons with me from 7 a.m. until 10 a.m.; assisting Harold with gardening from 10 a.m. until 11 a.m.; assisting Marlene with lunch preparations from 11 a.m. until noon; lunch promptly at noon; school lessons with me from 1 p.m. until 4 p.m.; assisting Marlene with dinner preparations from 4 p.m. until 5 p.m.; dinner promptly at 5 p.m.; household cleaning with Marlene from 6 p.m. until 7 p.m.; reading in the library from 7 p.m. until 8 p.m.; playing quietly in your room from 8 p.m. until 9 p.m.; bed time promptly at 9 p.m. and not a minute later. We do not own a television in this house. You do not need to worry yourself with matters of the outside world. You are safe here now and you should spend your time reading books to inspire your own thoughts, rather than dulling your senses with the needless drivel of television. Understood?"

She waits for my reaction. I swallow hard and smile awkwardly. "Yes, Grandma."

"Good. Now, on to the rules. First rule: you can enter any room you want at any time, except my bedroom, which is the master bedroom on the top floor. Under no circumstances are you to go in there. Second rule: you are never to leave the property at any time. It's for your safety. Third rule: you are never to ask questions about why we have not met until today. You will know the reason why in time, but not yet. Understood?"

"Yes, Grandma."

"You have that look in your eyes, Cindy dear, like you want to ask me a question."

"Um," I stammer. "You said something about my grandpa building this house. Who is my grandpa and where is he?"

Her eyes grow fiery for a moment with a startling fierceness. Then her eyes soften back to their brilliant blue color.

"An excellent question. Your beloved grandpa—Ernie was his name—is no longer with us. Unfortunately, the building of this splendid house took its toll on him and he fell ill, never to recover, after we had lived here only a few years. He lies buried not far from here." She pauses, swallows hard, and then continues without missing a beat. "Now, why don't you look under the bed for a very special gift?"

I gaze at her in wonder. Momentarily, I forget her comments about the dead grandpa I will never meet. The thought of another gift brings rapture to my face. Dashing for the bed, I shove my hand beneath the bed skirt and search with feverish excitement. My hand brushes against glossy paper. I pull out a boxed object wrapped in pink paper.

"Open it," she says, beaming.

After tearing the paper down the sides of the box, I work my fingers into the lid flaps. Prying open the lid, I stare down into the box, stunned.

"What do you think, my dear?"

The pink walls, the plush bed, the bookcase of books, and the full spread of new clothes and shoes are wiped blank in my mind. I see only the single doll lying against the bottom of the box, a freshly knit Raggedy Ann, straight from the store. Her head is in tact, her eyes are filled with life, and her smile shines like Grandma's, almost too strong to be real.

"She was your mother's favorite doll growing up, so I knew you would have to like her as well."

I feel my hands shaking slightly. I bury them into my lap, shielding them from her probing eyes.

"Thank you, Grandma. It's great." My voice is weak and airy.

"I'm glad you like her," she replies. "Well, on to the rest of the house we go. There is much to see, and I want you to be able to take it all in before it becomes dark. Once the darkness comes, we'll have to light candles in the rooms in order to see. It's tradition. You'll find out, soon enough. Come along. You won't need the doll now. She will still be here when you return later."

The sound of her robe grazing the floor as she sweeps out of the room tickles my ears. After taking a final glance at Raggedy Ann and her strange looking whole head, I stand up and follow Grandma into the hallway. My hands are still trembling as I trail behind her. Now I wish Mama was walking with me. I want to run back to my pink room and close that box, so Mama doesn't wander in there and see the new and improved Raggedy Ann, the better version that is supposed to replace the one Mama gave me. I hope she never sees it. The sight of the thing would simply kill her. As we leave the room, I blink and the image of Grandma leading me on to the rest of the mysterious house vanishes.

When I open my eyes, I realize it is later that night. The chirping of crickets buzzes in my ears with an irritating sensation. I am curled up beneath the pink covers of my new bed, as poor Raggedy Ann soaks up the sweat from my fingers like a sponge. She didn't seem nervous when we crawled into this soft but unfamiliar bed two hours ago, but I know my own anxiety is making her skittish.

My mind continues flashing from thought to thought, as if streaks of lightning are bolting across my brain. I can see each room Grandma showed me during the tour of this enormous place earlier today. Where Harold, the butler gardener, stays and where Marlene, the cook housecleaner, sleeps. Besides my pink bedroom and the rooms on the first level, each room on the upper floors seemed oddly uniform, almost a cookie cutter twin of the one beside it. A bed with a fluffy white comforter, a dark wooden rocking chair, and a matching dark wooden dresser and highboy fill each room in the exact arrangement of every other room.

The only difference between the rooms is a single item, which, as Grandma pointed out with emphasis, brings the room "distinct character." In one room, the "distinct character" was a custom Eiffel Tower miniature positioned proudly on the dresser top; in another room, an intricately woven rug from Peru; in another room, gold plated china dishes set against easels on top of the highboy. One particular "distinct character" item, which she seemed to highlight more than the others, was an ancient-looking marble chess set with finely crafted white and black pieces. The way she spoke about the chess set having "special meaning for the James women" made me wonder where it had come from and what exactly had happened to make it so significant. Maybe I will find out someday.

Every room has a purpose, she said, every room has a story and a reason for being here, a profound meaning from her life. The walls of the rooms were pale white, as are the hallway walls throughout the house. Even the two bathrooms on the opposite ends of each floor have white walls, white towels, and white countertops. The only room with any different color is my room. As we walked around, she rambled on about her and my dead grandpa hosting numerous families at one time, sort of like a hotel. Now Grandma must see the house as a homeless shelter since Mama and I have showed up.

As I explored the mansion in the daylight, it was a paradise unfolding with dazzling treasures and mysteries on each level. Now, in the darkness of the night, it feels more like a haunted house. There are strange insect sounds outside, the floors and the walls creak unexpectedly, and if it gets quiet enough, I swear someone is whispering something to someone else somewhere. Maybe Grandma and Mama are reuniting by playing a friendly game of "let's scare Cindy," pretending to be ghosts roaming the halls and uttering haunting noises that only my nightmares will remember.

I'm staring at the ceiling, not daring to breathe too loudly. I worry that if I look to the right side of the bed, I will see that brand new Raggedy Ann doll rise up out of the pink box with her fully attached head telling me it's time to hide under the bed because Daddy is coming down the hallway. I worry that if I look to the left side of the bed, I will see myself in that tall, oval mirror and find there is nothing worth seeing in the reflection—only an ugly, lonely girl who can't outgrow this dumb doll phase. Mama must be embarrassed of me, between my wasting her hard-earned McDonald's money by needing to buy pencils for school and my carrying around this headless Raggedy Ann like some stupid five-year-old. I wish I could talk to Mama, but now I feel like we'll never talk again or be as close as before because of Grandma—that lady is everywhere around here and she seems to cause Mama to shut down inside.

Tomorrow might bring something better, but this first night is scaring me to death. My lower lip keeps quivering and my eyes have water filling them, and even though I don't want to feel weak, I'm sensing the same heaviness I saw in Mama's eyes when we arrived this morning.

*Mama, I wish you were here with me. If I can't talk to you out loud and if your eyes won't speak to me anymore, then this will be my way of reaching you. I saw your expression darken when Grandma announced that I won't be attending public school anymore, saying she will become my teacher and this house will be my school from now on. Don't hide from me, Mama. I'm the only one who understands you; I'm the only one who understands us and what's happened. I know this is supposed to be a wonderful new place for us to live and have a great life, but the walls of this huge house are already squeezing the breath out of me. There's something lurking here that I want to forget before I've even had the chance to find out what it is.*

I close my eyes tightly, hoping sleep will find me, but knowing it will most likely elude me every night I will ever spend in this place.

I open my eyes to spot the half-filled journal page waiting in front of me. After setting the pen down onto the page, I lean back to lay my head on the inviting pillow. The candle still creates shadows on the walls and ceiling. The draft from the hallway outside still drifts into the room with unnerving intrusion. The same inability to sleep from that first night so many years ago still lingers like a disquieting ghost searching for rest it can never find.

# *Chapter Twelve*

"You've remembered quite a bit in a week."

With a soft whistle of amazement, Tony sets down the journal on the library end table and glances over at me. I can already sense the eerie lightness and heaviness in my limbs. The May afternoon sunshine struggles to peek in through the library window, failing to keep my slightly trembling limbs warm. He purses his lips, deep in thought, and drums his fingers on his kneecaps.

"Your Grandma was a piece of work."

I hold up my hands in self-absolution. "It's no wonder I'm so screwed up. It's in my bloodline."

He scratches his forehead and squints at me, as if trying to discern a secret I am hiding. "That's not what I meant. I don't believe you're screwed up. I think you're overwhelmed, and rightfully so."

I blink away water forming in my eyes. "This entire process is embarrassing."

He raises an eyebrow. "Why?"

"Because I'm a therapist. I should have realized there were potholes in my memory. I've spent years helping others find their potholes, but I missed my own."

He smiles knowingly. "It's perfectly natural to do that. In fact, it shows me that you're normal."

The word *normal* hangs in the air like a dangling carrot, taunting me with its nearness, something just beyond my grasp.

*Divert him, Cindy. Place the focus back on him; it's the only way to avoid his intrusive interrogation. You don't want him to know what's lurking in your mind, right? Then distract him. He's invading your privacy. Distract him!*

"So what would you do if you were in my position?" I ask, noticing the tremor creeping into my hands.

He shrugs. "I'd keep driving down the road until I found the potholes."

I bite my lower lip gingerly. "Even if they don't want to be found?"

"*Especially* if they don't want to be found."

I stare at him for longer than I should. "Thanks, Tony. You're making the hard parts a little easier for me."

He grins and leans forward in his chair. "Don't thank me yet. I have a feeling we're just scratching the surface. Do you trust me to take care of you?"

I look at him apprehensively. "What?"

He extends his hands in a calming gesture. "To be with you as you hit the potholes, that's all. I wasn't implying anything more."

"Oh," I say, my cheeks blushing. "Sorry, I—"

My eyes dart to my hands, which are trembling erratically now.

"No worries," he interjects. "Remember, you don't like me. You made that clear when we first met. I'm sure you have a 'no-relationship rule' with your patients anyway, right?"

"I—I—well—don't you?"

He gazes at me, causing my cheeks to redden again. "I'm seriously reconsidering it."

Our eye contact is broken by my hands, which are twitching unevenly like the fervent flapping of a bird's wings. I clench my fists to stifle the uneasy movement, while laughing nervously and veering my gaze toward the center room. Beads of sweat form on my forehead, as water stings my eyes.

I hear his offbeat voice speak gently. "We can stop for now."

Tears dribble down my cheeks as the uncontrollable vibration in my hands grows in intensity. Both arms wobble erratically, causing me to shift uncomfortably in the chair.

I look at him pleadingly. "I need to remember."

"Should I take you to the hospital?"

"No, just stay with me. It will pass once I remember."

My entire body jolts. The headache storms my temples with disorienting force. Within moments, I feel his arms around my quivering figure, gripping fiercely to hold me steady. His breath is hot on my face; his eyes arrest my terrified stare with stabilizing strength.

"I'm right here, Cindy."

"Ss—sorry—"

His arms clamp around my sides, while his hands press firmly against my back. "Stay with me," he whispers with alarm.

"I need—t—to remember," my voice sputters.

His face moves closer until our foreheads are touching. His stare captures my vision. "I'll be right here when you come back."

My eyes clamp shut.

My eyes snap open to witness her punishing gaze, unflinching in its pursuit of my nervous eyes. How Mama, with her quiet expressions and soft-spoken ways, was ever related to this powerful woman is beyond me. I dive my glance down onto the book page, desperate to avoid detection.

"Cindy dear, you must learn to read properly if you are to read at all. Do you understand? We have been in school for three months now. Have you learned nothing? This is not a difficult book. For a thirteen-year-old girl, your reading level should be much greater than it is. I will not ask you again to properly enunciate. I am your grandma after all, and I can deliver a swat to your bottom as quickly as I can deliver chocolate treats to your mouth. Do you understand?"

"Yes, Grandma," I answer, defeated.

"Now, try again and make sure you articulate your words and speak clearly when you speak to me. Once more."

I sigh as softly as I can, trying to suppress the flutter of anxiety in my stomach. After opening my mouth, I give her the best vocal strength I have never been taught to have: "'*And I pray one prayer—I repeat it till my tongue stiffens—Catherine Earnshaw, may you not rest as long as I am living; you said I killed you—haunt me, then! The murdered do haunt their murderers, I believe. I know that ghosts have wandered on earth. Be with me always—take any form—drive me mad! only do not leave me in this abyss, where I cannot find you! Oh, God! it is unutterable! I cannot live without my life! I cannot live without my soul!*'"

She waits for a moment and then smiles—that secretive smile she has mastered. "Much better, Cindy dear. Now, do you know what that passage means? Why did Ms. Brontë include it?"

My wary eyes swerve away from her, searching for the answer on the floor.

"Look at me. It's rude to look away from someone who is speaking to you."

I meet her forbidding gaze again, feeling the overwhelming weight of her knowledge, as if she understands something about me that even I do not know. "Because he's lonely?"

"At least you're thinking now. What do you make of Mr. Heathcliff's last line in that paragraph, '*I cannot live without my soul!*'?"

"Um—" I stammer.

"What's that? Quit mumbling incoherently. Speak up, for heaven's sake!"

Tears threaten my eyes. Trying my best to fend them off, I breathe hurriedly and spout out the first thing that pops into my head. "He feels haunted—by the thought of the love he lost. Now he's afraid he's losing himself and everything that's important to him. I don't know. I don't know, Grandma. I'm not smart and everyone knows I'm not smart. I can't do this."

Burning water rolls down my cheeks as I look at her helplessly. Her expression is unchanged, unmoved by my emotion. Those eyes staring into me feel like ice in my veins. She leans forward, while a smile sneaks up on her mouth.

"Don't worry, dear. I am here to teach you." Her voice lowers to a whisper, which oddly sounds as if it is surrounding me, creeping into my ears from all angles of the room. "It's a pity your mother never taught you how to learn, how to become your best self. I am here to provide you with all she has lacked in your life. Remember that. When you need, or want, or wonder, I am the one you are to come to, not her. You may love her all you can, but she is different from you and me. She does not have the spark of curiosity in her, the drive to question and to experience that which is beyond plain sight. Of course, she acted bravely to save you from your father and bring you to me, but her courage was fueled by fear, not strength. It is strength I will teach you. Your mother is weak. She lowers her head and obeys without questioning. You must find another path. Your freedom will come only by demonstrating your independence, and only if you follow my instruction will you discover this freedom. Do you understand?"

As I am entranced by her arresting gaze, I find myself uttering the words, "Yes, Grandma, I understand."

"Excellent," she responds cheerily. "Now, if you are good and do exactly as I say, someday I will tell you the secret of why we had never met until the day your mother brought you here. How does that sound?"

I hear myself answering robotically, "That sounds wonderful, Grandma."

"Splendid. With that in mind, our lesson is done for the day. You are making exceptional progress, and I am extremely proud of you, Cindy dear. When I am stern with you, it is only because I know how important it is for you to continue the family legacy as a woman of strength."

She pauses and examines my face closely. "You have that look again, like you want to ask me a question."

My fingers fumble over each other. Closing the book, I stare at the floor and rummage around in my brain for a question that would please her.

*Think, Cindy, think. A question that gets you what you want to know but also makes her feel important.*

I lean forward and lower my voice to a whisper. My hands are slightly trembling. *Just ask it, Cindy. You don't mean it, but you need to know. Mama will forgive you.* "How come you are so much stronger than Mama? Was there something that happened between you and her that made her realize how weak she was?"

Grandma's eyes sparkle.

*She's taken the bait. Now play dumb and soak in everything she says like a sponge.*

A supreme smile forms on her mouth. She seems confident that I will gladly forfeit my loyalty to Mama for the sake of becoming her disciple.

*I'm sorry, Mama, but if I am to survive in this house, then I will have to play her games and use her methods in order to find out what's hiding here.*

"Many years ago, your mother and I had an argument which brought out the worst in us. We lived in a small house, almost no bigger than this room, back when your mother's real father was in our lives. I suspect your mother has never mentioned him. Just as well. Anyway, your mother became upset because I was not willing to let her father run my life anymore. We left him and moved here. Sadly, she never allowed herself to find happiness in Sleepy Oak and ran away from home the day after she graduated from high school.

By that time, I had met your new grandpa and he had built this house for us to live in. It's so disheartening that your mother could not choose to be happy in this house. This is why I am so pleased that you are here now, so you can stay here through your life and someday have this house as your own, sharing in the legacy that I have for you to follow."

Her mouth goes silent, but her eyes continue communicating to me that there is far more to this story she will reveal to me as my days linger on in this place. I offer my best inquiring look and she nods.

"In time, Cindy dear, in time. All will be clear to you. For now, off you go. Find your mother, give her a hug, and tell her you love her. Even weak hearts need our love and affection, don't they?"

"Yes, Grandma."

"Now run along. Harold needs your help in the garden this afternoon. I'm giving you a fifteen-minute break right now to roam the house. Just remember where you are not to go."

"Yes, Grandma. I am not to go into your bedroom and I am not to leave the house property."

"Good. That's very good. Now come, give me a kiss, and then leave me to my reading."

I place the tattered copy of *Wuthering Heights* on the end table beside me. Then I hop off the chair, shuffle over to peck her freakishly tight-skinned cheek with my lips, and dash out of the library, struggling to steady my heartbeat. I sprint across the center room and up the stairs to my room as fast as my un-pretty legs can carry me.

The door is already open and I step inside, seeing Mama sitting on my bed, staring at the tall, oval mirror. In the reflection of the glass, I see myself moving closer to her from behind. She seems to be in such a daze that she does not notice me at first. I look closely at the mirror, observing for the first time how similar we are. I do not remember ever having looked at our faces side by side, but in this mirror, I can see the resemblance. There is the same quiet tragedy in our eyes of something horrific and unspoken. In this moment where she does not see me, I miss her more than I have ever missed her.

*If only you would look at me and speak to me, Mama. I need you to understand me—I need you to try. Please see me how you used to see me when it was only you and me. I can't be myself and live with me if you won't be yourself and show me how to live. Don't leave me alone with the woman downstairs; she's going to take what's left of us and destroy it. Look at me, Mama. Look at me!*

Suddenly, Mama's eyes lock onto my face. She comes out of her numbed trance and smiles, the weak kind of smile Grandma would pounce on.

"Hi, baby, I didn't see you there. Is everything all right?"

Blinking away tears, I smile back at her. "I'm fine, Mama. Totally fine."

"Come here," she beckons, patting the bed beside her.

I meander over to her and sit down. Together, we look into the mirror. I wonder if we will start making funny faces to lighten the mood, but I already know the answer to that question. Her heavy arm drapes around my shoulders and she pulls me tightly to her warm chest.

"I love you, baby."

"I love you too, Mama. Are you okay?"

She expels a weighty sigh. The deep inhalation lifts her chest and then releases it like an ocean wave rising and crashing onto the shore.

"I will be, baby. I will be."

Silence settles on us with a soothing calm. I wish we could stay like this for the rest of the day, just Mama and me, but I know she will have to let go of me and then I will not be able to rely on her for support or strength.

"Hey, Mama," I say, lowering my voice and pretending to be lost in thought.

"Yes, baby?"

"Why did we come here?"

The silence grows tense. "What do you mean?" she asks.

"When we left Daddy, why did we move here? I'm sure there were lots of different places we could have gone, but why did we end up here?"

This time, the sigh in her chest has a disturbing shakiness to it.

"I'll tell you someday, but not until you're ready."

I want to pry further, but her body grows rigid, telling me to let it go for now.

"Do you like your new room?" she asks absently.

"Yes, Mama," I answer, feeling her strong heartbeat.

"I got you something."

My eyes widen as she wrestles in her pocket and retrieves two Hershey's Kisses. She drops one into my outstretched hand and smiles with simple joy. I share the smile and glance from her chocolate to mine.

"Ready?" she asks, nudging me playfully with her elbow.

"You bet," I answer eagerly.

"One," she begins.

"Two," I reply.

"Three," we call in unison.

Then we dig open the wrappers and pop the treasures into our mouths, chewing like we're in a race. Our eyes sparkle with that sweet sensation.

"My favorite," Mama says.

"Me too," I chime in, ecstatic to see her happy.

"I'll be eating chocolate 'til the day I die," she says, her face beaming like the sun.

"Me too, Mama. Me too."

She pats my head affectionately. "I want to do something."

"What's that?"

Her left arm fumbles at her side and lifts up a camera.

"Let's take a picture of us in your new room."

"Okay."

Positioning the camera in front of us, she poises her finger on the picture button.

"Ready?"

"Yes, Mama."

Smile—click—flash. Then the moment is gone, something I'll hopefully have forever—even if only as a memory. She leans over to kiss my forehead, as she begins rising from the bed.

"I need to talk to Grandma. I'll see you in a little bit for lunch, okay, baby?"

"Okay, Mama. See you soon."

Mama lumbers out of the room, clutching the camera in her sweating hand. Then I'm alone, staring at my reflection in the tall, oval mirror. Without realizing it, I've stood up and I'm approaching the glass. My face appears grotesque to me, especially in the daylight where every oily inch of it is visible. As I gaze deeper into the mirror, I open my eyes wider, wondering if I should be alarmed at the blood trickling from my nose and the purple bruises forming on my cheeks. I open my mouth to call Mama, but then my face changes. A ghostly, pale color flushes over me, the skin transparent and lifeless. Terror claws at me; I sense it closing around me like the creaking walls of this house, ancient in memories, ageless in misery.

Then I look again and sigh with relief at my face which has returned to normal. Normal, yes, but still ugly. I want to cry, I want to feel Mama's presence. This place makes me feel lost from myself. I know I cannot stay here; I must find a way to get out. I shield my eyes with my hands, hoping to disappear in the dark.

As I open my eyes, I find Tony's face inches away from mine and feel his frantic grip around my shoulders. His eyes are swollen with concern. The trembling in my limbs has subsided.

He smiles. "Welcome back."

"I remembered more." My voice catches in my throat.

He releases me and steps back to survey my countenance. "Do you need to rest? Do you want me to call Jody and Samantha?"

I shoot him a cautious glance. "I don't want to burden them. This is too important to stop. I have to keep going. There's something at the root of all this, and I feel myself getting closer to it every time I find a memory."

"As long as you're willing to continue," he says, carefully scrutinizing my face for signs of weakness.

I begin massaging my temples with my fingers. "At this point, the episodes are going to happen whether I'm willing or not, so I might as well make some progress."

He allows a soothing silence to settle among us. Then he places a hand on my shoulder. "You're an amazing woman."

I look up at him and smile, taking in the warmth of his touch on my shoulder. Without warning myself ahead of time, I find my hand reaching up to touch his arm. My fingers move lightly, grazing his skin with tender movement. Our eyes share a sudden vulnerability.

"I trust you, Tony. Please don't make me regret it."

His gaze expresses an unyielding resolve, a tenacity to protect me and a longing to love me if I will allow it.

"I'll be here with you, Cindy, for as painful and as dark as it gets."

Tears threaten my eyes. "You'll stay with me through all of this?"

His eyes are resilient. "You won't be alone anymore."

My fingers fasten around his arm. "Are you sure you're ready? What if we're not prepared for what we find?"

The trademark grin forms on his mouth. "I'm all in. Now relax, I'll order some food, and then we'll jump back into the deep end."

I smile and slowly release his arm. As he begins moving away, he pulls his arm through my opened fingers until our hands connect and linger together for a few moments. He hovers thoughtfully, as if deciding whether or not to lean in for a kiss. His figure inches closer, while his eyes search mine for clearance.

I swallow hard, expel a quick gasp, and look away, withdrawing my hand from his. He pauses, perplexed, watching me bite my lip and fumble my hands together. Then he smiles and moves to the far end table to pick up the phone.

He looks in my general direction without making eye contact. "Is pizza okay?"

I glance out to the center room. "That's fine. Thanks."

# *Chapter Thirteen*

I open my eyes to find myself seated at the end of the massive dining room table, looking at the white frosted birthday cake and the fifteen lit candles spread across it. Grandma stands to my left, her eyes pointed and powerful, while Mama stands to my right, her eyes vacant. Harold and Marlene loom safely off to the side, grinning with pleasure.

"Make a wish, Cindy dear," Grandma commands.

*I wish to be free of this place someday soon.*

I lean forward and blow out the candles as quickly as possible, hoping it will please Grandma. I wish it was just Mama and me enjoying this cake in the beat up pickup truck on the way out of town.

They all applaud and then Harold and Marlene move to leave the room.

"A very happy birthday, Ms. James," Harold says stately. "Perhaps you might join me in the gazebo this afternoon—after I have finished my gardening duties, of course—and I'll teach you some of the card games I mentioned earlier this week."

"Okay, Harold. I'll see you soon."

He winks and disappears through the doorway.

"I hope you have a wonderful birthday," Marlene adds. "I'm preparing a special honey glazed ham and potato casserole for dinner." She smiles and then disappears as well.

It is only me and the mothers left. My pulse begins to race.

"Can we eat the cake now?" I ask, desperate to break the tension dividing me.

Grandma grunts. "I don't care for cake. And I don't suppose your mother would either, seeing that she needs to watch her figure."

I look up and watch Grandma's fiery gaze lock onto Mama's blank stare. Mama simply bites her lower lip and shakes her head.

"That settles it then," Grandma states firmly. "The cake is yours, Cindy dear. I suggest taking it to your room and eating it quietly by yourself. I have some afternoon napping to do, and I do not want to be disturbed. Do you like the cake I got for you?"

I glance up at Mama, hoping for a sign of recognition that I'm alive in her eyes, but there is nothing except emptiness. I sweep my eyes over to Grandma, whose penetrating gaze feels like a weight pressing me to the floor.

"Yes, Grandma. Thank you very much."

She seems appeased.

"May I be excused?" I ask hesitantly.

"Go ahead."

I grasp both sides of the cardboard tray supporting the cake and lift it off the table. Standing up, I look at Mama and smile. She sees me but offers no smile in return. Instead, she turns and leaves the room, scarcely making a sound with her retreating footsteps. I anxiously make a motion to follow her, but cringe inside at the sound of Grandma's voice again.

"Actually, Cindy dear, why don't you put that cake back down onto the table? I have something to tell you."

The sensation of shackles around my arms and ankles clamps over me. After gingerly placing the cake onto the table, I pull my hands to my side, sit down promptly, and give her my most convincing submissive expression.

"That's better," she says. "Now, without everyone else here—especially your mother—I can tell you the secret you've been waiting for since you arrived here two years ago."

She notices the intrigue crossing my face against my better reasoning.

*Don't be a pawn, Cindy. She's a master at this. Look at her, the conniving witch, drawing you in because she knows you care too much.*

"Okay, Grandma," I reply with interest.

*Be careful, Cindy.*

Grandma sits down on the chair nearest to me, so we are diagonal from each other. Her frame bends toward me.

*Don't let her touch you.*

I smile to keep her distracted as the rest of my body pretends to shift in my chair to become more comfortable, while actually scooting farther back in my seat away from her outstretched presence.

She appears oblivious, engrossed in the hidden truth she is about to reveal to my supposedly enraptured imagination. As her forearms settle delicately on the table, the look in her eyes changes to something sinister. Her voice comes out playfully, but with a wickedness lurking in its tone.

"Today is your day to hear the truth and join the ranks of the women in our family. After all, it's your fifteenth birthday, isn't it? You need to know what has been, so you can know how you are to be in the future."

I swallow hard and feel sweat forming on my forehead. Grandma's eyes pulse, as if revisiting some dark memory.

"Your mother and I have scarcely spoken, as you've no doubt witnessed, nor have we been as mother and daughter should be since it happened. I was once weak as she is now. I married a man who didn't love me, and I didn't love him either. It was a foolish mistake I regret every day, except it gave me your mother, who, in turn, gave me you. So for that alone, I am grateful."

At this, she pauses, giving me time to swallow her words. She begins slowly tapping her fingers on the tabletop, creating an eerie rhythm that sounds like a struggling heartbeat. "Your real grandfather was a vile, violent man. Beneath these clothes I wear the scars of his misdirected fury. Then one day, I fought back, not with my words, but with a large carving knife from the kitchen. It stopped him long enough for me to escape with your mother; in fact, it stopped his life altogether. Do you understand what I'm saying?"

I slide my quivering hands beneath my thighs. Biting my lower lip, I dart my eyes around the room, anywhere except to her face. "I think so," I say, my voice paper thin.

The terrible tapping of her fingers on the tabletop rises in volume, pounding my ears like the thumping heart beneath the floor in that Edgar Allan Poe short story, "The Tell-Tale Heart," that I read last year. Then her haunting voice slithers into my ears again. She waves her hand nonchalantly as if swatting away a fly. "Of course, we couldn't leave his body to be found, so I had your mother help me wrap him in garbage bags and bury him in the woods behind our property. She cried and cried, but I told her to stop those weak tears and pull herself together. We had to forget her evil father; we had to forget everything from before. People were never to know of what happened because it would threaten our safety. I made her swear to keep it our secret. By the next day, we had taken a bus across the country to end up here. We lived at the women's shelter downtown and I homeschooled her. I began using my maiden name, James, once more and promised myself that I would never change it again. Do you understand this, Cindy dear?"

I look at her numbly, while feeling my head nod and hearing my voice say, "Yes, Grandma."

*Don't let her touch you. Don't let her touch you.*

"I knew you would understand. This powerful history of weakness becoming strength runs like blood in your veins. Your mother will not accept this power, this responsibility. She was weak and could not even finish the necessary duty of ending your worthless father's life altogether. Your mother believes she showed mercy by allowing him to live, but all I see is weakness. Poor, pathetic creature. She does not have what it takes to be a woman of strength, a woman of true independence. But you will be different. You must never allow anyone who seeks to dominate you to survive, or else that person will own and control your life. If you give an abuser power, he will see to it that you have none. You must end him before he ends you. Understand?"

"Yes, Grandma," I answer hypnotically.

"Now, don't you feel special to be a James woman in this family legacy?"

I gulp. "Yes, Grandma. Thank you."

"So swear to me now that you will never tell a soul what you have been told."

I feel my throat closing up. "I swear, Grandma."

Her fingers cease their painful tapping on the table.

"Very good," she says, smiling as she would at a fellow conspirator. "So that is one of the family secrets. There are others, but you must earn the right to know them. In time, my dear, in time."

Her fiendish grin is nearly unbearable. She continues her speech, her alien blue eyes cutting through me like a dissection experiment.

"Within a month of arriving here in Sleepy Oak, I met, fell in love with, and soon married a charming man named Ernie Taylor. Ernie worked in the oil industry and was quite wealthy. He had this lavish house built for me as a magnificent wedding present. We lived here in happiness, except your mother, who continued brooding over the horrible days with her father."

She purses her lips and glances to the scenic countryside paintings on the walls, as if wishing she could transport herself into one of them.

"Once your mother ran away, we didn't speak for years. At one point, after Ernie had passed away, she sent a postcard with no return address, explaining that she had married a man who worked in a lumber yard. I responded with a letter asking where she was, asking her to call me immediately, but I did not hear from her again until another postcard with no return address came when you were born. Again, I begged her to allow me to see you, knowing you needed me in your life, but she kept me from you."

Grandma wipes tears from her eyes and avoids my gaze. "I arranged the pink room for you and changed it every year, buying new clothes and fashioning it suitable enough for a girl another year older on your birthday. But from the day your mother fled this happy house, the phone never rang, not once, for almost fifteen years, until the morning she called from a payphone to ask if you both could move in. Then, within an hour, you arrived at my doorstep— here for good, here to stay, here for life."

She pauses and waits for my response. The blood in my veins feels frozen. I shut my eyes, praying I will never have to open them and see her before me again.

My eyes blink and settle on an empty pizza box on the dining room table. Tony and I sit across from each other.

He looks at me earnestly. "So, what did you remember?"

I shrug and sigh. "Just Grandma confessing to me that she killed my grandfather and forced my mama to help her bury him in the woods behind their house."

His eyes widen in disbelief. "No kidding?"

"Unfortunately not. It was my fifteenth birthday. I remember feeling oddly relieved after she told me. Sure, it was a terrifying thought to have a murderer in the house, but it helped explain the tension between her and Mama."

Tony's face is incredulous. "Did Grandma's confession spark any conversation between you and your mom?"

"No, we still didn't speak."

He exhales heavily. "Amazing. You were only a teenager and you had to process the dirty family secrets all alone."

I nod stoically. "Every time I have a memory flash, I can recall more details of how I felt around the specific instance of the memory flash. I remember Mama being a closed book. It was strange how much we stopped communicating, how much we stopped seeing each other at all. The huge size of the house, combined with Grandma's sneaking me away for secret conversations about Mama's depression, created an environment where I was scared to go to Mama because I knew she was unreachable. All of life was funneled through Grandma, and she knew everything that was happening in the house at all times. Harold and Marlene were at her beck and call, and I was her puppet. I was never allowed to leave the house. I forgot what public school was like, what friends my own age were like, what anything outside was like. I was miserable, but there was no escaping, so I knew I had to make the best of it."

I take a breath, allowing him to digest the information.

"What else can you remember?" he asks, his eyes rapt.

"I remember that for a long time I would dream of my father and what had happened in our house growing up. Then I would wake up each night, sweating, hardly able to breathe. The only thing that pushed the memories out of my mind and allowed me to sleep again was convincing myself that the dreams weren't real. Making myself choose to forget something to the point of believing it wasn't true was easier than facing things about my life that I was ashamed of."

He furrows his brow, deep in thought. "So did your relationship with your grandma change after you heard her secret?"

"No, not at first," I answer, sensing the memory pull beginning to work on me again. "It only changed once she became sick."

"When was that?"

I sigh deeply. "I don't remember."

He raises an eyebrow. "How can you remember she became sick but not remember when it happened?"

I press my palms against my forehead. "I don't know. I just can't remember exactly."

"What was she sick with?"

"I don't know."

"Did she die from the sickness?"

"I don't know."

"But you know she was sick?"

"Yes."

"*How* do you know that?"

"I just know."

Tony chuckles. "Well, that's helpful. I think we need a break. I'm going to refill my coffee. Do you want some more?"

"No, thank you."

He snatches his coffee mug from the table and marches off toward the kitchen. My head continues throbbing intensely. I long for the comfort of his touch—his face pressing against mine, his arms holding me.

*Cindy, do not be weak enough to want him.*

My eyelids close, wondering where the darkness will take me.

# *Chapter Fourteen*

My eyelids open to a slew of unsightly weeds sprouting up from a patch of soil. Harold and I are on our hands and knees at the base of the garden, pulling the wiry green invaders from the ground and piling them into a garbage bag. The bulky work gloves itch and absorb the sweat from my hands. Harold takes a deep breath and leans back to wipe his forehead with his shirt sleeve.

"Mighty muggy day, Ms. James."

I smile at him. "Yes, it is."

He chuckles. "No matter what I spray on these weeds, they keep coming back every year. Stubborn things. Like bad memories that won't leave you."

I shed my work gloves and smear my grimy hands on my shirt. "Do you ever feel it's useless to pull them since they always grow up again?"

He glances at me and winks. "Good question, Ms. James. I suppose it keeps me honest, continually working at them. I wouldn't tend for the soil of the garden as much as I do if I didn't have to fend off the weeds. The good things that grow in here are better for it because of the constant care required."

"That makes sense, I guess."

We gaze out across the spacious backyard, listening to birds chirp about the weather and taking in the scent of the marigolds nearby. I slip my hands back into my gloves, knowing Grandma is probably watching from the house.

"Can I ask you a question, Harold?"

He uses a small hand shovel to hack away at a thick weed root. "Sure."

"How did you start working for Grandma?"

His eyes remain focused on the pesky root. "I was hired by Mr. Taylor when the house was first built. Twenty years travels awfully fast."

I mull over his words for a moment before reaching down to yank several small weeds from the dirt. "Do you like living here?"

His hands freeze, the shovel pausing in midair. Crouched over, he turns his head and looks me directly in the eyes.

"I simply live here, Ms. James, nothing more, nothing less."

I make a curious face at him. "But do you enjoy the house?"

A slight grimace crosses his expression as he sets the shovel down. "No more than I have to."

I lean closer, setting my hands on the ground to steady myself. "What do you mean? I don't understand."

He sighs heavily. "Is she watching us now?"

Slowly turning my head, I glance up to the top floor window—Grandma's bedroom window from which she usually watches us while we are gardening. She is nowhere to be seen.

"I don't think so," I whisper.

He lowers his voice until I can scarcely hear it. "I only stay here because it is safe for me, but this is not a good place for you to be. You need to escape if you can. Take your mother with you and find someplace far away where you can live. Now that you know what she did, I worry you will be around long enough to discover even more, and by that time, it will be too late."

Confusion crisscrosses my face. "I don't understand. How do you know what Grandma told me?"

His eyes swell with urgency. "Don't repeat a word of this to anyone. I've been around this place long enough to know far too much. You've only lived here for a couple years. The longer you stay, the harder it is to leave. Just get out if you can."

I warily glance back to the house. Grandma's figure stands in the top window. I close my eyes tightly to block her out.

When I open my eyes, I glance down at the massive kitchen countertop beneath me. Marlene, clad in her white apron, is busy dressing up the salads with cucumbers, tomatoes, cabbage, and Brussels sprouts.

"Cindy, honey, I believe that soup wants to be stirred." Her soothing alto voice permeates the kitchen with relaxed confidence.

I hop off the countertop and race over to the large stainless steel pot sending steam swirling like campfire smoke above the stove. I grip the spoon handle and make a wide circular motion, watching as the ham and pea soup mixes together.

"So, I was thinking we'd have some of my homemade panini sandwiches for lunch tomorrow, along with fresh grilled zucchini and squash, and then peach cobbler for dessert. How does that sound?"

My stomach rumbles. "Sounds wonderful."

The kitchen door jars open and Harold appears.

"She is on a tear this morning. I'd be careful if I were you."

Marlene and I nod soberly. Harold eases his way out of the kitchen and the door closes.

"Now, where was I?" Marlene comments to herself. "These potatoes are asking to be peeled. I better help them out."

She busies herself with the potatoes, while I continue stirring the soup methodically.

"Marlene, can I ask you a question?"

She keeps her face turned away from me. "Of course, honey. What's on your mind?"

"Are you happy here? With your life in this house?"

The slicing sound of the potato peeler grinding against the potato skin ceases. "Now that's an awfully complex question for a fifteen-year-old girl. What's made you so serious?"

I release the soup spoon and move over to Marlene's side, gazing up at her face. "I don't know. I think it's hard being here. I was just wondering if you felt the same way."

Her eyes dart over to mine, betraying their relaxed confidence for a moment. "Does this have to do with you escaping in here, hiding behind the refrigerator when you thought I wasn't looking, and trying to catch your breath so you could get back to normal? I saw you doing that a few days last week after lessons with your grandma. I'm on to your secret."

I fidget nervously, fumbling my hands over one another. "Sometimes I feel like I can't breathe. My insides are twisted up in knots, my head pounds like those migraines my mama gets, and my arms and legs want to twitch. I think there's something wrong with me."

She bites her lower lip tentatively and sighs. Placing the potato and potato peeler aside, she stretches her arm around my shoulders and gives me a tight squeeze. Her voice comes out in a whisper.

"I think you're fine, totally fine. And yes, I'm happy here, because you're here. But, as big as this house is, I know it isn't big enough for you, and, as Harold told you a few months ago, it would be best for you to get out in the world and escape this place. I'll miss my helper chef, but I hope you'll be able to leave sooner than later. I'm fulfilled because I have nowhere else to go, but you need more than this. You need your own life. So get out as quickly as you can."

Her eyes are rigidly serious. I watch her for a moment before closing my eyes.

My eyes open to see headless Raggedy Ann lying on my pink bed. I stare at her, remembering when we used to hold onto each other beneath my bed in the old house, warding off cockroaches with our tears.

A gentle knock sounds at my door. I glance into the tall, oval mirror to see Mama standing in the doorway. Her face is an odd mixture of worry and relief.

"Grandma's sick, baby. She wants to see you, but I told her you can't come to her yet."

Her eyes are alive, something that has been missing for so long that I forgot to look for it anymore. The fiery wildness in her expression is the same I saw on the day she stopped Daddy from hurting us.

"Where is Grandma?" I ask, my eyes darting around the room to see if she is hiding somewhere, listening.

"Harold had to take her to the hospital."

"How sick is she? What does she have?"

"It doesn't matter, baby. The point is she's not here today. That's what's important right now."

I look at her, puzzled. The unpredictable fierceness in her eyes is both haunting and intriguing.

*I'm glad you are finally looking at me, Mama, even if it is with that crazy, I'm-going-to-kill-someone expression.*

"What do you mean?"

She stares at me, trapping my gaze until I am fully aware that she has a secret of her own that she's ready to share with me. Our eyes communicate for the first time in almost three years.

*Yes, Mama, of course I'm with you.  Whatever you want, whatever happens, I've always been with you.*

With something resembling a mischievous smile, she raises her left hand and opens her closed fist.  Her palm faces upward, revealing a single silver key, an old skeleton key like the ones pictured in the illustrated pirate books I snuck away from the library to my room to read, the ones Grandma told me not to read.

"Follow me quickly," Mama says. Then she closes her fingers around the key, turns swiftly, and moves into the hallway.

Leaving Raggedy to fend for herself, I hop off my bed and scamper into the dimly lit hallway.  The late afternoon sun is setting somewhere beyond the tree line, making the illumination within the house fade and give way to shadows.  I silently trace each of Mama's footsteps to the stairs and then up two levels to the top floor. We creep with soft feet across the hallway until arriving at an unfamiliar, closed door.

I anxiously tug at Mama's shirt from behind.  She pauses and waits for me to speak, but she does not turn to face me.

"This is Grandma's room.  We're not supposed to go in there."  My sheepish voices trembles, making me feel weakness that Grandma would detest.

Mama's heavy frame sighs.  Her words are wispy, as hollow as the dead air around us.  "You're not going in there.  *I'm* going in there, and you just happen to be with me.  Now, we must be quick and quiet, understand?"

"Yes, Mama," I whisper.

I wait for Grandma's pronounced footsteps, for her arresting voice, for her penetrating eyes which glare with spine-tingling condescension. Nothing. Not a sound throughout the entire house.

*This is the only moment we will have to do this, Cindy.  Be brave. Mama needs you right now.*

After taking a quick breath to calm my nerves and reassure my mind, I watch as she inserts the skeleton key into the lock, turns the key until a dull thud sounds, and then twists the doorknob.  She pries open the door, sticks her head into the room, and surveys the scene.  Then she motions with her hand for me to follow and we step into the room together.

A massive bed sits on the wall to the right, covered by a purple comforter and silk pillows.  A wide wooden dresser, supporting a crystal encased mirror and various perfumes and jewelry boxes, rests on the wall to the left. A rocking chair leans on the back wall near the window. A plush cream colored rug lies beneath our feet, stretching in an expansive rectangle across the majority of the room's floor. Tall, freshly dusted wooden nightstands bookend either side of the bed. The finely decorated room seems posh and assuming, a reflection of Grandma's style and confidence.

Mama reaches behind me to close the door. Her eyes are tenacious, swerving back and forth across the room like an animal on the hunt. The suspense in her causes her figure to shudder slightly.

"Are you okay, Mama?" I ask, keeping my voice low.

"It should still be here. I'm sure she hasn't moved it." She speaks to herself, seeming blind to my presence.

I feel her brush past me on her way toward the bed. "Yes, yes, it must be here." Her voice is strangely monotone, as if entranced in its own numbed nightmare. Coming to the edge of the bed, she kneels down, careful not to ruffle any of the perfectly arranged bed covers. I watch her maneuver her sweat-covered arm beneath the bed. Then she bends even lower and appears to extend her arm upward to the underside of the box spring. Her eyes widen as her hand grasps something.

"I knew it would still be here," she murmurs to herself.

Upon pulling the object to her, she struggles to a standing position. Clutched in her hands is a wooden box nearly two feet long and a foot across. There are no markings on the box, only a narrow slit running along the side section that appears to be a lid. Mama's hands tremble as she holds the box. Her eyes look down at the object, seemingly lost in murky memories of terror.

"Open it," she says, scarcely audible.

"I don't want to, Mama," I answer, feeling the tremor in my own hands.

"You're sixteen years old, baby. It's time. You need to know."

I stretch my unsteady hands out to touch the wooden box. My moist fingers stick to the surface. Not allowing myself to wait for a reassuring breath, I lift the lid off the box and stare at the contents in amazed confusion.

Two thick carving knives, each coated with dried blood, lay side by side on a purple matted cloth. A wallet size picture of a man

I do not know is taped to the handle of each knife. The picture on the knife farthest from me is labeled *Dear Ernie Taylor*. The picture on the knife closest to me is labeled *Dear Paul Jeanetta*.

I stare at Mama in disoriented horror. Her eyes are sad, the fire from before extinguished by a lifetime of regret.

"Now you know, baby. She is not who she seems to be. You need to remember this and trust only me in the future. I'm so sorry." Tenderly, she reaches over, takes the lid from my hand, and places it back onto the box.

"I don't understand," I hear myself mutter. "She told me—"

"She lied to you, baby. She's not right in her mind. Yes, she killed my daddy, Paul, in self-defense, but she didn't tell you about killing Ernie, her second husband, which means she lied to you. She killed my daddy because she had to, but she killed Ernie because she wanted to."

The breath in my chest feels cut short. A harsh burning sensation fills my eyes with tears. I feel my feet inching backward. "Why did you bring me here, Mama? Why did we come to live here when you knew what she did? I don't understand. Why, Mama?"

She looks at me resolutely. "It was the only safe place for us."

"This is your idea of safe?" I hear the tone in my voice rising.

"She'll never hurt you, honey. She'll never hurt me. I knew that. We'll be safe here, no matter how disturbed she becomes in her mind. All she wanted was her freedom, to do as she pleased. When she felt that was compromised, she made the obstacles go away. She had been living here, having her own way for years. She wanted her family back, so I knew we could at least have a home here."

"But look what she's done, Mama. How can you not see this as wrong?"

"I do, baby. But it's not as easy for me. Surely you can understand. I brought you here so you could have a life I could never give you. I've tried to take care of you. I have to worry about your well-being."

"Then why did you bring me here to the psycho's house?" Now my voice is ringing in my ears.

"Don't talk to me that way, baby."

I feel rage empowering me to say what I want to restrain myself from saying. "Why, are you going to take one of these knives and gut me with it, the way you did to Daddy?"

Unspeakable agony surfaces on her face. "I'm warning you, baby, let it go. I don't want to hear you speak of that again. Everything I've done has been for your good."

"Grandma told me you're weak," I say sharply, as tears begin trickling down my cheeks. "She said you're not a good mother. I see now she was right."

Mama's eyes reassume the foggy pain I have grown accustomed to seeing for the past three years. Her eyes no longer want to speak to me. A distinct isolation the size of this house moves rapidly to separate us, yearning to bury our memories in these unforgiving walls.

"I'm sorry, Mama, I didn't mean it," I say unsteadily. "I just don't understand what's going on. Please help me understand."

Her eyes are silent, unwilling to find me. With sealed lips, she hands me the box, as if it contains the unwanted shards of her heart, and walks to the door. I see her open the door and slip outside into the darkness, leaving me burdened with the wooden box and the family history trapped within it. I close my eyes to hide them from the sight of it.

I open my eyes to see Tony standing over me, holding my head in his hands. A look of worry covers his face. The strength of his grip on my scalp is unnerving at first, but I realize he is only trying to support my slumping head and body.

"What—happened?" I ask, hearing the distinct slur in my words.

"Another episode," he answers, exerting effort to raise my figure from the tabletop and rest me against the back of the chair.

"The memories—they—keep—coming," my mouth sputters.

"I know, I know. Can you feel your arms and legs?"

"For the most part," I answer, keeping my eyes focused on his to gain composure.

"Can I please take you to the hospital now?"

"No—no," I reply quickly in my mind, though the sound comes out labored. "I just need to get upstairs. I'll come back to normal if I can sleep. If we go to the hospital, they'll only run more tests, find nothing, and tell me to watch my stress and go home to rest."

"All right," he says, placing his hand on my sweaty forehead. "But if you get worse, I'm taking you straight to the hospital. I'll be sleeping down here tonight. I'm going to lift you up and take you to your bed, okay?"

"Okay," I slur back to him, feeling my consciousness already ebbing.

He pulls the chair away from the table and slides his arms beneath me, shifting and adjusting their position to secure my body. Then the sensation of freefalling sweeps over me, as if being raised in my figure but plummeting in my mind simultaneously. I close my eyes, blocking out the blurriness in my vision. The jarring thump of his footsteps reverberates through me as I am moved across, then up, then across, then down.

The welcoming softness of bed sheets enfolds me. Covers are spread across my torso, followed by a cold washcloth being applied to and then removed from my clammy forehead. Before slipping into dreams, I remember the touch of a comforting hand brushing stringy hair out of my eyes and gracing my face with uncommon tenderness I do not recall ever experiencing before.

# *Chapter Fifteen*

*Mama, do you remember that tall, oval mirror I used to have in my pink room? It's been on my mind a lot lately. I'm remembering my reflection in it, and I fear it will never change. That same frightened, ugly girl will remain frozen in time, staring at her own face with dread, realizing she is cursed. Only darkness and death wait in her future.*

*So I need to know, is it possible to change my reflection? Can I become someone truly alive, or is a ghost the only image left for me?*

It is the dead of night. The shadows have no room to tempt or taunt, for all is dark. Yet I know this house without seeing it. Raggedy Ann clings to me, her headless figure trembling against my throbbing chest. The candles within each room are strangely unlit tonight. The eerie silence lies with suffocating clarity across the levels.

Raggedy Ann and I stand at the banister on the top level, overlooking the void. How easily I could climb this railing and release myself. How splendid the graceful fall will feel. I would take Raggedy Ann with me. We could end this together, discovering the bottom, the final memory of this misery.

Perhaps later tonight, I conclude, pulling myself away from the ledge after observing the man wrapped in blankets and sleeping soundly in the middle of the center room floor. I make my way quietly across the hallway, down two levels, across another hallway, and into the red room.

As I enter the room, the urge to crawl down onto the floor, curl up, and weep calls out to me, but I do not have the will in me tonight to cry over this place. A final glance around the dark room reveals the same nothingness stewing within me.

*It's time to give in to the darkness, Cindy.*

*I'm not ready. Please give me more time.*

*You've wasted your years already. I've been patient enough.*

*Now bury these fleeting feelings and finish it.*
*But Tony. But my memory. But my future.*
*All gone, sweet, stupid Cindy. All gone. Nothing remains*
*for you but the abyss. Mama knew this. Why do you think she didn't fight it?*
*She wanted to live!*
*Her mind was weak, just like yours. Like marbles scattering on the*
*floor, Cindy. Soon you'll lose them all.*
*Please, just a little more time. I can change. There's hope for me.*
*Your hope died the day you were born. Don't be a fool. Stop resisting*
*what you know you want. Be a woman of strength, a woman of independence.*
*Climb the banister. Let yourself fall. It's time to come home.*
*No, Cindy, don't listen to her. You know you don't want this.*
*Listen to me, Cindy. I know you're tired of fighting. Give up. That's*
*it. You are a James woman, here for good, here to stay, here for life. Here, in the*
*abyss.*

As I turn to head out of the room toward my relief, I hear a familiar voice I have only heard in my dreams. It's Mama's voice, echoing softly throughout the room.

*Stay with me. I'm still here, baby girl. Stay with me. I'm still here.*
*I'm always here.*

Tears trickle down my face in the darkness, spilling at my feet. I stand watching, waiting for her embrace. I close my eyes and remember her eyes, hoping they can still see me.

All I feel until I leave the room two hours later is Mama's presence—cradling me, lulling me to rest, and pulling me with all of her might away from the abyss.

*** 

I open my eyes to see a man sitting on the rocking chair at the far corner of the room, waiting for me to awaken. The blurriness in my sight dissipates with a few blinks. I sense the warmth of several blankets covering me from above, while the cushioning mattress greets me from below. After yawning groggily, I test my limbs for activity, finding gratefully that I have full function of my arms and legs. My eyes scan the room, noticing there is no candle burning by the drapes. My gaze drifts back to his face.

"This is a first for me," Tony says. "I've never slept over at a patient's house."

"Sorry," I say, pleasantly surprised at the non-slurring strength in my voice.

"How are you feeling?" he asks, his eyes probing me.

"Well enough, all things considered. Your therapy is brutal."

He grins. "That's fair. Since you're finally awake, I'll go to the kitchen to find breakfast."

He makes a motion to rise from his chair.

"Why are you doing this?" I ask suddenly, startled by my own question.

He turns his head back toward me, appearing caught off guard. "I need to get some food in you. You'll need strength to stay well."

My eyes refuse to release him. I sit up and lean against the sturdy wooden headboard. "Why did you race over here the other night, break down my door, and rush me off to the hospital like a person trying to redeem himself? And why are you so intent on tending to me now?"

He sighs, glances away, and reaches to the floor beside him. His hand lifts up a slew of sample pill packets and waves them back and forth like a scolding teacher.

"These are dangerous, Cindy. You shouldn't be taking these. You know that."

My stare remains undeterred. "Please answer my question. Why do you care so much? What are you hiding?" I swallow hard and bite my lower lip tentatively. "Tony, I like you more than I want to, but I need to know, what makes you feel so responsible for me?"

Strangely, tears fill his eyes. He folds his arms, looks away from me, and focuses on the wall. He seems to be traveling away to a pain living somewhere I cannot follow.

"I had a patient kill herself," he says abruptly. His words quiver with emotion. "It was at my last practice. She first came to me for stress management. The more sessions we had, the more it became clear she probably needed psychiatric help beyond what I could give her. But she was also overly dramatic and wanted attention. I didn't make the referral to a psychiatrist because I thought it would only make her more flamboyant in efforts to get someone to embrace her theatrics. So even after she came to me during our last session and begged me to help her because she was worried about what she might do to herself, I told her she would be fine and simply penciled in another session for the following week. The next day, I found out she had overdosed on antidepressants. She swallowed three bottles worth and locked herself in her bathroom so no one could help her."

He looks over at me, yet remains fixed in the memory. "I couldn't even attend the funeral, I was so ashamed. I tried to go back to work, but every time I sat in my office, I pictured her sitting on the sofa across from me, pleading with me to help her. The thought of what I had done, or not done, consumed me. So I quit the practice and relocated here based on the recommendation of John Shipper. I thought this would give me a fresh start. When my first patient came in, I was so nervous that I started making jokes to lighten my own mood. The humor seemed to relax the patient, so I tried it again with the next patient. Then, before I knew it, I had adopted this entirely new method of therapy which was so unlike me—casual, carefree, personable. It helped me cope with my guilt, and it helped the patients feel calm enough to be vulnerable. It was invigorating to feel like I could recreate myself in a new place."

He clears his throat and exhales slowly, still wary of making eye contact.

"A few days later, John called me about your situation. When you walked into my office, I saw the same pain on your face that I saw in that lady's face—the lady I didn't help. I wanted you to know that I understood you, even before we knew each other. But I thought you needed some light-heartedness instead, so I kept up the act. If there was any possible way for me to help you, I was willing to do it. That's why I came immediately the other night. I had to make it right. I had to help this time in a way I didn't before. Reaching you was my first and only thought. Not just to redeem myself, but because from the first thirty minutes I spent with you, I knew there wasn't any possible way for us to keep living without being in each other's life."

He grows quiet, engulfed in his thoughts. The water glossing his eyes begins to drip freely, rippling down his cheeks. "You may not have wanted me, but you needed someone. And I needed someone too."

He bites his lower lip pensively and then releases a tired sigh. My heart urges me to stand up, walk over to him, and pull him close, but I remain motionless. He quickly rises from the chair and heads toward the doorway.

"I better see about that breakfast," he murmurs, trying to keep his face shielded from mine.

I watch him walk through the open doorway and around the corner.

*Let him walk away, Cindy. You can't afford to become drawn in—you know where that leads. Think of Grandma. Think of Mama. Self-preservation is your only freedom. Focus on his negative qualities. Think with your head; don't feel with your heart. Your heart is fickle and weak-willed, like Mama's. Don't listen to it; it will only betray you and leave you defenseless. Let him leave. You don't need him. You don't want him. You shouldn't want him. You won't survive if you become weak enough to want him.*

\*\*\*

My bare feet tiptoe across the center room floor, stopping at the kitchen double doors. My body pauses, waiting for my mind to make its decision. A few anxious breaths leave my lungs, colliding in my chest with the frantically pulsing heartbeat sending my nerves abuzz. After jarring open the door, I peek my head around the corner to see Tony, with his back turned to me, busy frying an omelet in a pan on the stove top. With a cautious push, I open the door wider and step into the kitchen.

"I was wondering when you'd come," he says in a casual tone.

"I was curious to see what you were up to," I reply, hoping the waver in my voice is only obvious to me.

He turns around to face me, his eyes bright and inviting. "I'm glad you came. This is quite a kitchen. Far too large for only one person."

My insides flutter as I move closer to him. He turns back to the stove and uses the spatula to flip the omelet over in the pan. I come to his side and keep my eyes fixed on his face. He looks over at me and smiles.

"Do you like omelets?"

I simply nod. A lightness fills me, tickling my insides with nervous excitement. "Thank you for staying with me through this. You can't understand what it means to me to have you here."

He glances down at the omelet. "My story isn't scaring you off?"

"No. Is mine scaring you off?"

He furrows his brow pensively. "No. Do you think less of me for what I did?"

I place my hand on his arm. "I think more of you because you told me."

He turns his head fully, gazing at me intently. We stare at each other for a moment. Our heads slowly lean toward one another. Then, without warning, we both withdraw, acting aloof and uninterested.

"So I take that as a *yes*, you like omelets?" he comments with noticeable shyness in his voice.

"Yes, I like omelets."

"Good, because if you didn't, I'd feel incredibly stupid right now."

A breathless pause dashes between us. Then our eyes find each other again. He clicks the stove off and gazes at me. Without warning, I find myself lunging forward, my lips connecting with his. I suddenly feel drawn in, a purity and beauty passing between us in the simple, strong kiss. Our lips linger for a few seconds, sharing a fervent passion, before I release him abruptly.

I expel a rushed breath. "I'm sorry. I don't think I can do this."

His eyes are murky with confusion. "Then why did you?"

"Impulse. I shouldn't have. I can't get involved right now."

He touches my hand lightly. "It was just a kiss, Cindy, not a marriage proposal."

I glance into his eyes, finding the comforting calm of his expression trying to reassure me. My eyes dart to the floor.

"This was a bad idea. I abused the vulnerability of the moment and I apologize."

He inches closer and extends his hand to raise my chin so that our eyes are level. "I didn't share my story so that you'd kiss me. I shared because I felt safe to share. We both have some healing to do."

His hands move to hold my face softly. With a slow lean toward me, he presses his lips upon mine. A desperate fierceness courses between us. His lips let go and his face looms like a stabilizing presence.  My arms enfold him, one hand clamping onto his sturdy shoulder and the other hanging onto his neck.  The unshaven stubble on his cheek brushes against the tender skin of my face, the sensation both natural and soothing.

"I need to trust you," I whisper in his ear.  "I need you to let me trust you."

His grip around my trembling figure tightens.  He presses his face to mine and then allows our foreheads to rest gently against each other.  His voice is steady and deliberate.  "You can trust me.  You can believe I will watch over you.  And you can love me."

The tears dripping from my eyes are close enough to splash onto his face.  My hands grasp the sides of his head.  I kiss him firmly, feeling my lips and my heart afire.

"I know," I whisper.  "And I do."

# Chapter Sixteen

"You did *what?*" Jody exclaims, slapping her hands on the checker top diner table.

"You told him you loved him?" Samantha chimes in next to me.

"It was totally unexpected," I answer, smiling and blushing.

"How did this happen?" Jody stammers. "He didn't take advantage of you while you were temporarily paralyzed, did he? I'll kill him."

I laugh and shake my head. "No, of course not. We were together at my house and it just happened."

Jody whistles as her eyes widen. "This changes everything, honey. He's no longer your therapist; he's your man."

I nod slowly, biting my lip pensively. "I can handle that."

Samantha pats my arm. "I'm proud of you, Cindy. He seems wonderful."

I scratch my fingers on the tabletop and dart my eyes between their glowing faces. As the moments pass, my thoughts begin drifting away from Tony and toward the rolling thunderclouds of memory once again. An unsettling truth stirs within me, the realization that these carefree get-togethers with Jody and Samantha at the '50s diner have merely been an escape from reality, a way to avoid revealing the trauma of therapy. Every week, we sip our milkshakes, shoot the breeze, and lose ourselves in this idyllic atmosphere, but all these trappings have become my method of keeping my secrets hidden from them, the best friends with whom I should have been sharing my struggle this whole time.

After shaking off the cloudy disturbance in my thoughts, I paste a smile on my lips again and perk up my expression. "Tony's not what I wanted before. He conforms to none of my wish lists.

Yet he's the perfect non-convention for me. I don't understand it, but I don't need to understand it this time."

Their eyes swell with amazement.

Jody leans forward. "You *do* love him."

I nod swiftly, an enraptured smile bursting across my mouth, conveniently sweeping away the haunting thunderclouds until after we have gone our separate ways.

***

"So I assume you broke the news to the ladies today," his pleasant voice slips into my ear.

"It came up in conversation," I reply, shifting my shoulder to reposition the phone against my ear. I prop myself up, trying to get comfortable against the pillow-padded headboard.

"How are you feeling about everything?"

"Surprisingly fine. I miss you," I say, darting my eyes over to the window area, verifying that I remembered to light the candle beside the drapes.

"I miss you too."

A pleasant pause settles among us.

"So how was your day?"

He chuckles. "Far too busy. I'm still at the office, compiling notes on my last patient."

"It's almost 10 p.m. I didn't know you were such a workaholic."

"Am I jeopardizing your stereotype of me? Sorry about that."

I can picture him smiling.

"How long will you be working tonight?"

"Quite a while. A lot of catching up to do."

"So I guess I'll see you tomorrow." The tone in my voice hangs hesitantly.

"Cindy, I can hear you thinking over the phone. What is it you really want to say?"

I laugh nervously. "I don't know. Maybe you could come over—and I'll make you a late dinner. When you're done, you know?"

A lingering silence follows. I bite my lip and hold my breath.

"I'll be over in twenty minutes," he answers before hanging up the phone.

***

Ten minutes have passed, and I still cannot will myself to crawl out bed, peel off my pajamas to get dressed, and tend to dinner. My hands are folded in my lap. The quiet of the house is oddly comforting. For the first time I can remember, peace has flooded my thoughts, allowing me to risk a hopeful dream rather than face a haunting darkness.

In my mind's eye, I picture a simple ranch style white house on a spread of land far from here. A porch swing hangs invitingly near the front door, a tire swing hovers with playful ease from a thick maple tree in the backyard, a grill sizzles with tantalizing barbeque scents, and a freshly cut springtime lawn shakes off winter's death grip and brings new breath into the lungs. In the middle of this serene scene is a happy family enjoying a breezy afternoon beneath a sunlit sky.

Tony and I sit beside each other on lawn chairs, letting our bare feet linger leisurely in the cushioning grass. We hold hands and whisper sweet nothings to each other, those cliché phrases of affection that actually mean something profound for us. Being next to him and feeling the security of the silver bond on my ring finger provides a contentedness that my mind cannot fully fathom; only my heart truly understands it.

A few feet ahead of us, joyfully camped waist deep in water filling a bright green inflatable pool, is our daughter. She has dark curls, wet and wild, tufting around her tiny head. That beautiful face, fashioned with Tony's olive eyes and narrow nose, yet balanced by my freckles and fair skin, is indeed an image of us together. The innocence in her toddler eyes is a sweetness I will savor for the rest of my life. As she splashes and screams with delight, I feel as though I might shed sublime tears, or maybe even melt into the lawn chair with utter bliss. My body is so relaxed, my heart is so fulfilled, my mind is so peaceful. I am in my place, the place I am supposed to be, the place I never have to leave.

The image scatters in my mind, forcing me against my will back into the solitude of my bedroom. My hands tense, warming with perspiration. The sense of abandonment nags my thoughts. As I sit unmoving on the bed, a distinct dread worms its way through the peaceful notions of a moment ago, decaying the dream into a lifeless shell. A terrifying realization strikes: I am in my place, the place I am supposed to be, the place I can never leave.

The darkness expands in my mind, causing the worry to weave like a spider's web around my heart, ensnaring, wrapping in silk bondage, and suspending me for a late night snack to be devoured by its poisoning jaws. The fear is paralyzing, elbowing out pleasant dreams of being with Tony and our daughter and replacing them with suffocating questions of what will happen when my strength to resist the legacy runs out.

Will there be a time when I can no longer realize I should even be fighting for a healthy-minded future because I'm already plunged into the nightmarish reality of twisted thinking, believing all the while that insane Cindy is actually sane Cindy? Normal thoughts of wanting to see the man I love, wanting to be near him and feel his touch, wanting to share life together—these thoughts are what I worry can never be normal to me because of the illness ticking like an internal clock down to mental implosion.

The nagging *what ifs* grate against my reasoning, bending the breadth of what a regular woman should be content with—the standard hopes and dreams of health and love and joy—and breaking me like a branch to be tossed into the fire of derangement. What if Tony only loves me because his goal is to fix me? What if Grandma's and Mama's madness is lurking in my head, a venomous, coiled snake ready to strike at any moment? What if the curse will never be lifted, but instead will be ever lingering, ever growing, ever reaching up to pull me off the cliff of sanity and into the abyss where I'll disappear with Grandma and Mama and all the other women who have gone before them, these tragic James ghosts?

*You're nothing but a ghost, Cindy. Your mind will soon be forfeit to senility and suicide.*

*No, I'm still here. I'm still real, not a shadow of something real. I'm not gone yet. My mind is not broken. You don't own me, and you can't have me. Leave me alone.*

*Yes, alone, that's what you are. That's what you've always been. Completely. Alone.*

*Please go away. I don't want you here anymore.*

*Sweet, stupid Cindy.    That's exactly what Mama and Grandma thought about you every day.   They didn't want you.   Nobody wants you.*

*I don't—believe—I—can't—*

*What, are you crying now?   How weak.   Pathetic.   You are a disappointment.   You don't have what it takes to be a James woman.   But if you surrender to the abyss, you'll find your strength yet.   You'll find your peace, your freedom.*

*No, I won't do it.*

*No one will miss you.   No one cares about you.   They only want to fix you, not love you.   Just let yourself slip into the void.   It's easier, trust me.*

*No!*

*You worthless wretch!   You are weak!*

*I want to live!*

*Your life is not worth living!   Your only value is in dying.*

*I will keep running, I will keep fighting, I will keep breathing.*

*Very well.   Do as you will, but when you're exhausted and can't run, fight, or breathe anymore, I'll be waiting.   Sooner or later, you'll give in to the darkness.   All the women in your family do.   It's in your blood, girl.   It's in your brain.*

*Get me out of here!*

My eyes burst open to a tiny hospital room.   I wonder if I have been led into the wrong place.   Surely this is not her room; I do not recognize the shriveled shell of a person at all.

"I would say twenty-four hours at most," a confident doctor's voice echoes from the hallway.   I wait to hear the sound of sobbing, but Mama takes the news in silence.

I inch forward, mesmerized by what I assume is the form of Grandma.   The tight skin of her face sags with weathered wrinkles, appearing to have been let loose like a clothes pin unclasping a drying dish towel from a suspended line.   Her typical blonde dye job lays half-matted, half-frizzed on her scalp, the yellow color removed and replaced with a dirty snow shade.   No elaborate, elegant robe or outfit covers her anorexic-looking figure—only a thin, off-white hospital gown.

Most changed of all is the magnitude of her eyes.   Instead of sparkling with overpowering mystique, they now appear hollow, as if two holes have been drilled into a mannequin's plastic head, just enough to let light come into the face from the outside but giving no light from within.   Those black hole eyes are silent, no longer taunting my mind and terrifying my heart; they are only circular gaps in a skull which can no longer own me.

"If we would have located the tumor earlier," the doctor's voice enters my ears again, "perhaps we could have tried an invasive surgery, but there was no time once we did find it. I'm so very sorry, but the aggressive nature of a brain tumor, especially when it's discovered this late, often means a short time frame, as is the case with your mother."

Mama responds with no questions, no tears, no anything. Her silence thunders in my ears, making me feel guilty for moving to Grandma's side. Yet I know I need these few moments—probably the last I will ever have with her—to close and seal shut a door somewhere within myself. How odd that what I hoped for, though never in this way, has happened, yet it brings me no comfort to be free. I will miss being near her, despite the truth that I hardly wanted her near me.

Grandma's empty eyes roll over to see me standing beside her. The chapped lips of her mouth attempt in vain to create a smile. I smile for her and place my moist, burning hand on her cold, veiny hand.

"I'm dying—Cindy dear," she speaks dryly, her voice crackling like interrupting static on a radio station.

"I know, Grandma," I reply, patting her hand, hoping the memory of this moment will not haunt me in my dreams tonight.

"I love you—very much—and I have always wanted what's best for you," her words struggle out of her mouth.

"I know, Grandma. I know."

She takes a deep breath, which causes her to cough wretchedly. Then she looks me in the eyes for the first and only time during my visit. "Give your mother a hug for me and tell her that I love her."

The doctor's voice rambles on from the hallway. Grandma glances in Mama's direction, making sure that she is distracted, and then lowers her voice to an eerie whisper. "I will stay with you, even when I'm gone. Don't be weak and don't give in to the weak. Listen only to yourself now. It's the only way to survive. Remember what I've told you, even if she tells you it's wrong. You know who was stronger. I love you, Cindy dear. Before I met you, I did. And after

I've passed, I will. The house will become yours. Make it your home, and I'll never be too far from you."

Another throaty cough causes her to gag. I wait for the fit to pass, but the hacking seizes her body fiercely. Within moments, I see the doctor, a kind-looking gray haired man, moving to my side to help her. A firm hand grips my shoulder and draws me away from the dying old woman. I want to turn and cling to Mama, but I also want her to know I'm still angry with her, so I stand still and allow her the privilege of keeping her hand tightly pressed against my shoulder. For the next several minutes, we stand in silence, Mama watching me, me watching Grandma. We watch her cough, we watch her writhe in pain, and then we watch the breath leave her lungs for the last time. I close my eyes and feel the tears dribble down in silence.

I open my eyes to watch cold rain plummeting from the gray-streaked sky, soaking my black dress and causing it to stick to my shivering skin. Mama and I stand beside each other, neither of us making a motion to embrace or console the other. Instead, our tearless eyes blink away water splashing against our eyelids from above, as we stare in numbed indifference at the casket being lowered into the muddy earth.

Marlene and Harold watch from nearby with stoic expressions, concealing any emotions that might be stewing within them. The minister, a middle-aged man with thinning brown hair and a pudgy face, attempts to shield his Bible from the monsoon while reciting comfortless verbiage from its water smudged pages. The two gravesite workers are busy lowering the casket to the exact six-foot depth with the crank machine. The wooden box reaches the bottom and the workers cease their efforts, trying their best to be sensitive to the moment.

I hear the minister's tone drawing to the end of a question. "Would any of you like to say something about Cindy to pay your respects?"

I look at him in shock.

Then I snap back to awareness, fidgeting with my hands and fixing my gaze on the casket below.

"Would any of you like to say something about Elaine to pay your respects?"

Complete silence. The only sound is the pattering of rain colliding with foreheads, shoulders, feet, and gravestones. The minister peers at Mama, waiting. Nothing. Her eyes neither look at him nor at the coffin below. He switches his gaze to me. I answer him with distant eyes.

"Very well. May she rest in peace," he proclaims quietly.

Without further ado, the man closes his Bible, nods, and begins moving away from the gravesite. Marlene and Howard speak quietly to each other and then turn to leave as well. After another minute of unresponsive quietude from us, the workers grasp their shovels and begin unearthing soggy ground and flinging it onto the casket.

Mama and I wait for what seems like an eternity as the workers fill the gaping hole with earth until it can be filled no further. We watch them express their condolences to us with somber head nods before they climb to the top of the graveyard to escape past the thick black gate. Then we stand and allow the rain to continue washing us, cleansing us. I ignore both the water squishing between my shoes and the feeling of pruned skin covering my body, looking at last over to her face. Her eyes are filled with anguish.

I slide my frigid fingers into her palm. She closes her fingers around my fingers. We begin leaving the gravesite without speaking a word to each other. With labored steps, we silently climb the grass-soaked hill toward the black gate. A combination of freedom and dependence swirls within me as we move. It is as though an understanding of what just happened settles in to my senses. Her death brings the independence I have craved, but the creeping cords of a legacy being passed down have already coiled around me and feel as though they will only tighten their grip with each hour, each day, each year, until I am suffocated and dropped into a gaping hole, filled and completely swallowed in darkness. As we move past the black gate, I grip Mama's hand fiercely and close my eyes.

I open my eyes to see Tony entering my bedroom, a concerned expression covering his face.

"Hi, beautiful," he says with a nervous smile. "How are you?"

My eyes are melancholy. "I was remembering again. Sorry about dinner."

"No worries. Where did you go?"

I sigh and glance away. "Grandma's funeral."

He comes to sit on the edge of the bed. "Do you want to talk about it?"

I avoid his gaze and fold and unfold my hands with compulsion. "No, not this time."

I can feel the intensity of his stare. He strokes the side of my face with his hand. "But talking it through will help you process the memory. If you want to stop the episodes—"

"I'm fine," I interject more sharply than intended, jerking my face away from his hand. "I don't think we need to talk about my memories anymore. I'm fine."

He reaches over and pats my hand. "The more you keep saying you're fine, the less I keep believing you."

I sigh with exasperation. "Please leave me alone about it."

He grunts and looks away. "You need to be honest with yourself, Cindy. Have you been taking your medicine?"

I pause for a moment, allowing my expression to change from defensive to coy. I tease his arm playfully with my fingers.

"Of course. I'm fine."

I stroke the side of his face in return and attempt to pull him in for a kiss. He reaches up to stop me and grasps my left wrist, his fingers coming to rest on a rippled, irregular protrusion of skin.

"What's this?" he asks, his eyes moving to the scar.

"Nothing."

"How come I've never seen this before?"

I sigh heavily and glance away. "I'm usually wearing a watch over it."

"What is it from?"

I close my eyes instinctively. "I don't want to talk anymore. No more memories."

I hear him moan, exasperated, and I know he is looking at me with disappointment.

"When will you want to talk, Cindy?"

"Not now," I repeat quietly. "Please leave me alone. I need space, time for myself. I'm done for a while. I'm sorry. Leave me alone."

I slip off the bed and race into the bathroom, hoping to hide the tears threatening my eyes.

# *Chapter Seventeen*

Our steps take us along the grassy stretch beside the gravel path winding from the broken water fountain to the main road at the end of the driveway. The humid June air lingers like a saturated cloth on my skin.

"I'm glad you finally let me see you again," Tony says, trying to act casual.

"I needed time to process."

"I know. Just promise me something."

I shoot him a cautious glance. "What?"

"Don't ever make me wait another month before being allowed to see you again."

I smile nervously. "I won't. I'm sorry. You'd be pleased to know I threw out the sample pills I got from Jody. They were only making things worse."

"I'm glad," he answers quickly, as if worried I will change my mind. "They definitely accentuated the episodes. We can't afford that."

After nodding perfunctorily, I fidget with my hands.

"Anyway," he adds without missing a beat. "I've been mulling over what you said to me in the kitchen a few weeks ago."

As we move, our hands graze each other. Finally, he reaches out and interlocks his fingers between mine, holding my hand securely.

I smile at him. "What's your conclusion?"

He scratches his hairline with his free hand and glances at me with honest eyes. "I forgot to answer you."

The buzz of my nerves rises in hopeful anticipation. "What?"

He stops and turns to face me, using his free hand to hold my other hand.

"I trust you," he says candidly.

His eyes watch for a reaction.

I stare at him, wondering, waiting.

Then he smiles. "And I love you too."

He leans forward and kisses me tenderly. Upon releasing my lips, he surveys my countenance thoughtfully.

"I didn't expect this," he says at last. "I thought you despised me."

"I did." I smile and squeeze his hands. "But you wore me down with chocolate."

He grins supremely. "Beautiful."

We turn and continue our stroll along the winding driveway.

I glance over to observe his demeanor transition into therapy mode. "So, after Grandma passed away, there was the funeral and then what? Do you remember what came next?"

"No," I answer, scrunching my forehead. "I've had a block since the night of the last episode. I know Mama died somehow, but I can't remember exactly what led up to it. The strange thing is I recall being away from this place while in college. Every memory except the ones that happened here in this house is still available, but the ones involving this place are dark and gone from me. Isn't that bizarre?"

"Not if the memories from here don't want to come back. You know how trauma works; your mind has a way of storing it up and locking away, as if it didn't exist at all. We just have to find some type of association so you can bring it out of the dark."

I expel a deep, shaky breath. "I'm scared to find out what's there."

He grasps my hand once again. "We'll keep walking through this together, memory by memory. Okay?"

I bite my lower lip and then whisper, "Okay."

"Do you remember what happened the day you and your mom got back from the gravesite? Did you talk about the carving knives under Grandma's bed, or what you would do for school with Grandma gone, or what Grandma said about you getting the house? Anything?"

My mind flashes to the pink walls of my bedroom. I see myself staring fixedly at the walls, my face reddening with anger.

*Keep him out, Cindy. You don't need him, you don't want him. Stay safe within yourself.*

"I don't remember—" I say, my voice trailing off.

He looks at me, doubtful.

In my mind, I see Mama's presence entering the room from behind me. I glance at the tall, oval mirror to see her reflection: the hunched over shoulders, the sad countenance, the empty eyes. I watch her and my spite rises.

*Distract him. Anything to divert his attention. Get him off the trail.*

"Nothing at all?" he asks.

"No," I answer with more edge than I intended. I turn to him abruptly, as he looks at me curiously. I clench his hand tightly and use my other hand to stroke the side of his face.

"We're wasting our day off, Tony. Let's go get lunch."

I offer him my best flirtatious gaze. He appears to be lured in at first, but then he flinches as if waking from a trance.

"Nice try," he says with a smirk. "But you underestimate my bull crap radar. If you are too tired to talk, that's fine. If you honestly can't remember anything, that's also fine. But if you *can* remember, and you simply don't want to revisit what you're remembering, then don't use seduction as a decoy. I'll gladly be with you, but only if it's because you want to be with me, not because you want to use me as a distraction in order to avoid the truth of yourself."

I pull my hand away from his face. "I told you, I don't remember. I need lunch."

I turn back toward the house and walk away from him as quickly as my fatigued legs can carry me.

Only two steps away from entering the house, I blink and find myself in the pink walled room. I resist the urge to cry and turn instead to face Mama, my expression smoldering. Her vacant stare has nothing to say in response.

"What are we going to do now, Mama?" The harshness in my voice is unnerving, but it's her fault if she takes offense to it. "Grandma's dead, Harold and Marlene are gone because you don't want them around anymore, and I'm supposed to be a junior in high school, but I've only passed the seventh grade in real school. How am I going to graduate from high school? Why didn't you speak up and make Grandma send me to a public school when we first got here? How are we going to live in this house? We don't have any money; you don't have a job; we have nothing, Mama."

Her heavy frame heaves with a sigh and she lumbers over to the bed. "I don't know, baby, but we'll make it. We have to make it. Grandma left us some money to use. We'll send you to a school in town. I'm sure they have tests you can take to pass the grades you've missed. You're smart, baby, you can do it."

Tears rise in my eyes. "I don't want to do this, Mama. I don't know anybody my age. I don't have any friends. Can't we sell this house and move somewhere else to start over again? I'm afraid to stay here."

Now her eyes light with a peculiar fire. "Baby, *this* is our home. We came here to live and this is where we have to be. We have nowhere else to go and no other family to turn to."

"But I hate it here. Can't we leave already?"

"No," she answers firmly.

My eyes plead with her. "Please, Mama. Let's sell the house and leave. Grandma can't keep us here anymore. She said the house would be mine. Can *I* sell it?"

Mama's eyes grow quiet again, shrouded in dark thoughts. "No," she repeats, almost in a whisper.

My lower lip quivers. "Why did you hate Grandma? She loved you, I know it. But you never loved her. She wanted to give me things you never could, but you hated her for it. She was strong, Mama, stronger than you'll ever be. I wish you were like Grandma, because she wanted what was best for me. I don't think you want what's best for me anymore. I guess Grandma was right. You *are* too weak to make the right decisions, your heart will never be strong, and you'll be stuck in this place forever. No wonder Daddy beat on you; you were an easy target."

Her hand lashes out and strikes my cheek. The fire erupts in her eyes, the same savage wildness I saw on the day she stopped Daddy cold in a pool of blood. "Don't you *ever* speak to me like that again, Cindy Jeanetta James!" her voice bellows.

I am so shocked by the force of the blow and the power of her voice and presence that I am stunned into silence. Tears drip from my eyes and splash onto my arms.

"I will say this once and I will never say it again," she says, her voice hushed to a menacing whisper. "I hurt your daddy because he was a terrible man who did terrible things. I hurt him because it was the first time he had ever threatened to hurt you, and I knew he really would hurt you. But I didn't kill him because I didn't want you to see that and have to live with it. That's why I didn't kill him; it was for you."

Her words catch in her throat for a moment, causing her to swallow hard and brush tears away. "And I loved your grandma more than you will ever understand, but she was the kind of woman I never wanted to be—the kind of woman I hope you won't want to become. I brought you here because I wanted you to know her. You deserved that much. But there is something she kept going in this family that has to end with you. You had to see it for yourself to know why I did what I did and to understand that your life can be different. I want more for you, baby. This house will be yours to own once you turn twenty-five, based on Grandma's will, and then you can sell it if you want to. Until then, we have to stay here because this is all we have. It's better this way, though, because now we can start over, just us. No Daddy, no Grandma, just you and me, baby."

I still feel the sting on my cheek. My teeth grit together and I sneer at her. "I don't want this house, I don't want this life, and I don't want this family! You may as well have killed her yourself. Go ahead, Mama, hit me again if you want. It'll be right in line with the family legacy, right?"

Her eyes are shocked, anguished. I want to retract the words immediately, but they remain floating in the air of my pink walled room, ready to be repeated in her mind over and over. I open my mouth to apologize, but she is already turning away and heading for the hallway.

*Let her leave, Cindy. You don't need her. You don't want her. The only freedom you can have is in being independent. Don't let your guard down and don't be weak, or else you'll end up like her.*

I watch her disappear around the corner and into the dark hallway. My puffy eyes scan the walls of my room, disgusted with the cheery pink color. This house has no more room for pink. There is only one color to match the kind of family that lives here.

*That's it, Cindy. Let her leave. Let her leave you alone.*

I blink and the room disappears.

I blink and my wobbly step lands in front of the closed double doors. Gaining my bearings, I turn around to find Tony rushing toward me.

"Easy there," he cautions, extending his hands to balance me. "What just happened?"

"I remembered something again."

"Let's get you inside."

***

"Checkmate," Tony says with a juvenile grin, reaching down to knock over my queen.

"That's two in a row," I huff.

"Don't worry, I'm keeping track."

"Gloating is unbecoming," I say, folding my arms.

"So is losing," he replies, flashing his teeth.

We share a smile, sitting across from each other on the library floor with Grandma's ancient marble chess set spread between us. The chess set is the only item of Grandma's "distinct character" collection that has remained in the house all these years, the only item that does not seem haunting to remember. I adjust my Indian-style position, leaning to either side to work out stiffened muscles. Tony begins resetting the chess pieces.

"So," he muses, "any more health issues?"

I scratch my fingernails against the marble edge. "Not since you asked me twenty minutes ago, and not since the twenty minutes before that."

"This is a good day then?"

I pat his hand. "You can stop worrying. No shakes, no tremors, no temporary paralysis. Just chess with my man. I'd say it's a good day."

He waits for me to continue, but I simply glance at him and shrug. He nods and finishes resetting the finely chiseled white and black pieces into their square battle positions.

"Tomorrow might be different," I add at last.

He hums to himself and drums his fingers on his kneecaps to the rhythm in his head. "But *today* is a good day."

I scratch my fingernails on the marble once more. "Yes, and that's all I can hope for right now. It's been a few days since my last memory, so maybe I'm tapped out for a while. I'd be grateful for the rest. Remembering is a full contact sport for me."

He grins. "Your move."

I inch a black pawn ahead two spaces. "Thanks for the house arrest date, by the way."

"My pleasure," he replies, mirroring my move with his own white pawn. "Although you better start winning, or else I'm going to have to take my gaming skills to another party."

"Shut up," I say, jabbing his kneecap with my fingernail.

"Ouch. Please confine your fighting to the chess board only," he mock pleads, holding up his hands in self-defense.

I laugh and scoot another pawn forward. "I call house rules, meaning I can use any method necessary to win."

His eyes dance. "What exactly does that mean, Ms. James?"

I spring from my sitting posture, crawl around the chess set, and plant a forceful kiss on him. He loses his balance for a moment, overtaken. Then, I release him, snatch his white king, and roll it across the hardwood floor. He peers at me, mystified. I simply smile.

"Checkmate."

# *Chapter Eighteen*

No evidence is left of the panini sandwiches on the empty paper plates. We sit next to each other on the plush couch in the library, my head resting on his chest and our hands interlocked. The steady rise and fall of his breathing comforts me. If only the constancy of his presence could banish the inconsistency of my memory. I sigh contentedly and grip his hand tighter.

"I like this kind of therapy," I say, raising my head from him and leaning it against the back of the couch.

He chuckles. "Me too."

He drums his fingers on his kneecaps. Our eyes play cat and mouse for a few moments. I lean into him, offering my lips to break the tension. He returns the kiss and strokes hair out of my face.

"I still can't believe you live in this house," he comments, as if the topic has been nagging at him all day.

"How romantic," I reply.

He grins sheepishly, ceasing his finger drumming. "Sorry, it's just difficult for me to grasp."

I linger my face close to his, yet I feel my mind already careening backwards. Clearing my throat, I smile, almost as an act of apology.

"Do you think I'm crazy, Tony?"

"To be with me? Of course not. I'd like to think I'm perfectly normal—"

"You know what I mean," I interrupt, smirking at him. "Do you think I'm crazy?"

He blows a sigh out of the side of his mouth, away from my face. "I think you would be crazy to continue the way you had been living—lost without remembering much of who you were. But I don't think you're crazy for wanting to find yourself."

"Do you think I could lose my mind?"

He smiles and kisses my forehead. "We all could lose our minds. That's the risk of living."

We sit in silence, not making eye contact. I perceive his elusive replies to indicate that he will not give me a straight answer, no matter how I ask the question, so I allow the subject to fall away harmlessly.

"The bad thing happened here," I say distantly. "I can feel it. But I can't see it yet."

"It'll come. Just give it time. It's here somewhere."

I fold my arms and lean back to gain a better view of him. After a reassuring breath, I smile dryly. "Okay, I'm ready. I feel memories stirring again. I need to visit them while they're fresh."

"Are you sure? It's been a couple weeks since the last flashback. I don't want you to bring on another health episode by forcing it."

I grip his hand and squeeze tenaciously. "This is the only way forward. So hit me."

He nods and snaps into therapy mode, his eyes alight with penetrating tenacity.

"Tell me about the house after Grandma died, about how the house affected you and your mother. Describe the atmosphere. Immerse yourself in that environment."

I nod and look across the library, the picture starting to come into focus. "It always felt lonely. Once Grandma passed, the smothering depression covered every inch of the house like a predictable fog rolling in. Mama's darkness deepened, causing her to be paranoid constantly. She moved into Grandma's old room, had double locks installed on the bedroom door, and started isolating herself, keeping everything out, including me."

The memory flash sneaks up and takes me in an instant.

I open my eyes to find myself racing out of Mama's bedroom and barreling down the hallway on the top floor of the house. I can sense Mama's heavy figure close at my heels.

"No, Mama, not this time!" I say, gritting my teeth.

"You listen to me, Cindy. I'm your Mama!" she insists, her voice shaky and desperate.

"I'm tired of you being depressed," I plead.

I feel her slick hand grasp my arm and turn me to face her. I glower at her and hoist up the damning evidence: a plastic bag filled with several orange bottles which are nearly empty.

"Do you know what you're doing to yourself?"

She huffs at me, her eyes glassy. "I *need* them, baby. Give those to your Mama."

I shake my head decisively. "Painkillers, antidepressants, sleep aids, all jumbled together. You've got a death mix in here."

"You shut up now, baby girl," she yelps, flailing in vain for the plastic bag.

I yank the bag beyond her reach and rattle its contents furiously. "You don't need these. They only make you worse. Please, let me throw these away. Come out of your fog, Mama. I need *you*, not some pill popper who's numb to everything."

Her eyes grow panicked. "No," her voice says coldly.

"You're losing your mind, Mama. Can't you see that?"

Now she sneers and fastens her arms around my shoulders, jarring my thin frame as if I weighed no more than Raggedy Ann.

"You don't understand," she strains. "It's not something I can stop. It's the only way I can keep living."

"You have a choice, Mama."

"It's not that easy—"

"You're being weak, just like Grandma said. It's all in your head."

She pushes me away roughly. "Shut your mouth, young lady!"

Tears burst in my eyes. "Why are you giving in to this? Why won't you fight it?" She stares at me, lost. Then my blood boils, rushing redness to my face. "I'm not going to give in to it when I'm older. I'm going to fight it, Mama. I won't be weak like you."

Her expression softens with sadness.

"You'll understand one day," she says, gasping for breath.

"No, I never will," I snarl back. "I won't be like you, you'll see. I'll never be like you."

She takes in my words grimly. "Give me those pills, Cindy Jeanetta James, or so help me—"

I hide the bag behind my back and try a new tactic.

"Fine, Mama. You'll get these pills back if I get to paint my room something other than pink."

Now the darkness returns to her eyes. She laughs strangely, the laugh of a person without all the marbles secure in the head. Her voice is low and defeating. "Never."

"Fine!" I yell, heaving the bag into the vast opening between the levels.

We watch as the plastic parachute does little to stifle the bag's momentum. The pill package plummets to land on the center room floor with a piercing popping sound that echoes through the levels like popcorn kernels bursting in a microwave. Mama is so awestruck that it takes her a few moments to look at me, her face gnarled with rage.

"Go get it, Cindy," she demands icily.

"Get it yourself, Mama," I answer, darting away from her and descending the staircase to the third level.

I shout, "And just so you know, I'm leaving this house forever on the day I graduate from high school," before slamming my bedroom door shut behind me.

I open my eyes to see Tony waiting anxiously. I grimace and hold my hands palms up.

"Another fight with my Mama. This one was about her pill addiction. I don't know why neither of us made an effort to reach out and reconcile, but I'm sure we knew it was impossible by the time I left. If only I could remember—there was something significant that happened—I can feel it in me somewhere, something horrible. Every memory that comes back to me brings it closer, but I still can't find it in my mind."

He places his elbows on the table, folds his hands together in front of his face, and rests his chin atop his interlocked fingers. "Maybe it happened when you left?"

"No."

"Maybe when you came back."

*Don't answer that. Keep your mouth shut.*

"I don't know. No, I definitely don't know."

He looks at me, perplexed and intrigued. "Now there's a sly reply."

"What?" I counter with a smirk. "I can't remember. Why do you keep thinking I'm lying to you?"

"I might believe you if you were a better liar. Now, come on, Cindy, whatever is coming back to you has to be dealt with.

Pretend you're in the room by yourself. I'm not even here. Close your eyes and go back there."

I sigh and glance away from him. "I don't think—"

"Cindy," he. says, grasping my hands. "Seeing as how you could scarcely stand to be in my presence for the first few hours we knew each other, the very least you can do is pretend I'm not here and ignore me for a few minutes. Is that too much to ask?"

I catch myself smiling. "I guess not."

"Good," he says, squeezing my hands for reassurance. "You can do this."

I stare at him, my eyes growing wide.

I see a blurry image of myself standing in the center room, feeling the firm wooden floor beneath me.

"Let yourself go there," his voice says distantly.

My eyes open to find Mama blocking my exit to the front double doors. Her eyes are a mix of desperation and despair. A backpack stuffed to the brim lies at my feet.

"You can't do this, baby. Don't do this to me." Her pathetic voice grates in my ears.

"I'm not doing this to *you*, Mama. I'm doing this for *me*. I have to get out of this place. Why can't you understand? How can you want to stay here?"

I see the sweat gleaming on her forehead. Her hands are fidgeting with anxiety. "This is our home. You can't leave me here alone. You're eighteen now, baby. Only a few more years and you can have this house as your own. You can repaint your room any color you want, I promise. Just stay here. We can stay here together. I *need* to stay."

I huff in exasperation. "And I need to leave. There's nothing for me here but bad memories, Mama. Why are you making this so difficult?"

She steps forward and extends her arms as if to embrace me, a gesture I sense is actually an effort to impede my escape. I take a step back from her advance.

"Listen to me, baby," her weak voice pleads. "If you go out there, you're gonna have a hard life. It's safe in here. I'll keep you safe. Understand?"

"No, Mama, I don't understand. That's why I have to go. I need to find something more for myself. I've stayed as long as I could take it, but I can't do it anymore. I'll come back to visit you, I promise, but I'm never going to live here again."

She lowers her arms and stares at me, lost. The five-year chasm fitting into the two-foot space between us feels unbearable. I hold up my hands in a truce and then take the first step toward her. She takes the second step and we enfold each other in a painful embrace.

"Sorry, Mama. I love you."

"I love you too, baby. You call me, when you want to, and even when you don't want to, okay? Just call me—just call me."

"Yes, Mama. I will."

"Here, this will help get you started." I feel a thick wad of folded paper being pushed into my pants pocket.

"What this?" I ask, releasing her.

My hand reaches for my pocket, but she places her hand on my hand to stop my progress.

"Don't look at it. Just take it. Do good with it. You take care of yourself. Be better than me, baby. Be better than me."

Our eyes lock and my heart feels ready to burst. My mind tells me I should move, but my feet remain frozen in place.

"Go ahead, baby. You don't want to be late."

I nod, remembering again why the backpack is lying at my feet. Then I lean down, scoop it up, sling it onto my shoulder, and step toward the open front doors.

"I'll visit. I promise. See you soon, Mama."

I catch her eyes for the last time, finding their heavy sadness sending tears trickling down her cheeks.

"See you someday, baby," her voice whispers, scarcely audible.

I turn my face toward the doorway to shield my falling tears from her and quickly exit the house to the taxi waiting at the circle drive.

I open my eyes and look at Tony, feeling a catch in my chest. As I expel a heavy sigh, I sense water collecting in my eyes. He reaches over to pat my hand gently.

"Did you find it?"

I shake my head. "No, but I'm getting closer."

"So where did you go?"

"Here, seventeen years ago, when I left home. I took off and left Mama here by herself. She had given me several thousand dollars to get started. I ended up in Kansas City and landed a clerical job at a CBT practice, which turned into something more substantial as I earned my bachelor's and master's degrees along the way. Seven years passed and I hadn't come back to visit her like I promised I would. This place was too haunting, and, as I read in her letters— which I soon started leaving on my desk unopened—Mama's depression deepened. She had started cleaning the house chronically, compulsively—and losing her grip on reality."

"So when did you come back?" he asks earnestly.

I close my eyes as the memory flash tugs at me.

The phone is ringing. I am picking up the receiver and placing it to my ear, already dreading the conversation to come.

"Hi, Mama."

"Hi, baby. Sorry to bother you. It's just we haven't spoken in a long time."

"No problem," I say, forcibly light. "I've been meaning to call you."

Her silence lingers. She knows I'm lying; I can hear it in her anxious breathing.

"Just wanted to check up on you to see if you're okay." Her tone is wounded, as if struck by a punishing blow.

"I'm fine. Totally fine, Mama."

"Good, good," she mutters, as if to herself. "I'm so glad to hear it. How's work and school?"

"Busy, busy," I say abruptly, rummaging through some papers on my desk top, knowing the conversation, as usual, will drag on with awkward pauses and trite phrases, allowing me time to multi-task. The mood grows heavy again. I jot some notes on a homework assignment to distract myself, but the void of silence aches in my ear.

"The winter weather has been lovely here in Sleepy Oak," she says expectantly. "The snow is beautiful, and there's no ice, so the roads are clear for traveling."

I roll my eyes and cover the phone mouthpiece with my hand to muffle a heavy sigh. "Sorry, Mama, I won't be able to come home for Christmas this year. I have several assignments to finish before my master's graduation in two days, and work has been busier than usual because of extra holiday stress for patients. Too much to do."

A lengthy pause fills the line. I cringe and begin massaging my forehead with my free hand, hoping it can assuage the guilt.

"I know," she says quietly. "I know."

"But I'm definitely going to make it next year," I add hastily, knowing it sounds overly eager and inauthentic.

"I miss you," her voice wavers.

"Miss you too, Mama."

Distancing silence fills the phone for another several moments. I go back to filing paperwork on my desk, coming across a rubber-banded pile of unopened letters from her, which I promptly cover with other papers. Then, without warning, I find myself speaking rapidly, desperate to dispel the unbearable tension.

"How's the house cleaning going, Mama? I know it's a monster to maintain. Did you get the repair man to come fix the weather strips on the back doors that you were telling me broke loose last year? There must be frightful drafts of cold air coming in. Have you gotten outside to see Christmas lights? I hope Grandma's Cadillac still works. Any new restaurants downtown? Maybe we could eat at one someday. So what else is new with you? Hope your health is good. Things are going well here. It's nice to be in a big city. So much to do. But, as I said, I'm always busy. No time for anything else, you know?"

I pause, catching my breath, feeling my body tremble with anxiety. A tired sigh drifts into my ear. Something like soft sobbing comes through the phone.

"I'm sorry you're so busy, honey," she says weightily. "I was just wondering if you might be able to come visit me for a couple days. Maybe just one day if you don't have any more time than that."

"But Mama, I already told you that I'm busy—"

"It's cancer, Cindy."

I release the papers I have been organizing and slump down in my desk chair. My mind begins spinning with a flurry of converging images: her bloodied nose and bruised face; sitting beside her in Daddy's red pickup truck; blowing out my birthday candles and watching her leave the room without eating a slice of cake; embracing her before leaving the house on my way to catch the taxi that will drive me away to freedom in Kansas City.

"Oh, Mama—" I whisper. "I'm so sorry."

"That's all right, baby. I only have a few months left. I just wanted to see your face and hug you before it's over."

"I'll be there, Mama. I'm leaving to come to you as soon as I walk off the stage at graduation commencement."

My eyes close to restrain freefalling tears.

My eyes open to see Tony's face again.

He smiles sadly. "So you came back."

I nod and swallow hard. "I came back. She was sick, and she needed me."

"And what do you remember after that?"

The image of a bloodied carving knife stuck into a pink wall flashes across my mind. I stare at him with vacant eyes. "Nothing. Nothing at all."

I rise from the couch and make my way into the center room, heading toward the kitchen, leaving behind what must be his perplexed expression.

## *Chapter Nineteen*

Elvis is insistent about a rocking party at the jailhouse. Their mouths are running a mile a minute between sips of milkshakes, while I am using all my energies not to focus on the image of a bloody carving knife in my thoughts. The atmosphere is abuzz with midday clamor from surrounding customers and chipper waitresses rattling off the lunch specials.

"So have you talked about the future with him?" Jody chirps.

I shift in my seat uneasily. "No, not yet." I glance around distractedly. Then I realize they are staring at me, puzzled. "Sorry," I mumble, "just a lot going on around here. Anyway, what was I saying? Oh yes, we're still trying to solve the riddle of my memory. For the time being, I'm content knowing he's with me in the midst of it."

Samantha shakes her head and raises her eyebrows in amazement. "A lifetime of protective armor undone in a few months of unorthodox therapy. Incredible."

We sip our milkshakes in silence for a few moments. I sense the trauma of the last therapy session worming its way into my mind, distorting my present concentration.

Jody perks up. "What if you can't find what you're looking for in your mind? Will the episodes ever stop?"

An awkward pause fills up the table. My eyes, which have been roving around the diner, return to their faces. "What was that?" I ask.

"I said will the episodes ever stop if you can't remember what you need to?" Jody's tone is sharper, but edged with concern, not irritation.

I smile nervously. "I—I—don't know. Right now, I can only focus on trying to remember. I have to believe I can get better.

Remembering is the key. If I don't believe I will remember all that I need to find, then it's hopeless."

Another silence lingers.

Samantha leans forward eagerly, as if unable to contain a secret any longer. "Guess what you'll never believe? Carl's going to an AA meeting."

My eyes widen in disbelief. "How did this happen?"

An earnest grin bursts across her mouth. "I gave him an ultimatum. I told him if he didn't get sober, I was going to leave him. I even had a bag packed and everything. He came home drunk, I confronted him, and then I stormed out of the house, just like Jody suggested for dramatic effect. It worked better than I'd hoped. He followed me out of the house, slurred an apology, and even shed a few tears—my favorite part—before saying he would go to the first meeting available. I can't believe I'm going to get my husband back."

I muster a supportive smile. "That's wonderful, Samantha. I'm thrilled for you."

Her demeanor exudes newfound confidence. "It's because of you. You said I was worth it, and I finally believe it. Now he can get better and we can have a new start."

Jody grabs her milkshake glass and raises it. "Here's to impossibilities coming true in all of our lives."

Samantha and I raise our glasses to Jody's and we clink them together, our faces beaming. For a moment, the dark cloud hanging over my thoughts vanishes. Even as the depressive force begins returning a few minutes later, I cover it with the brightest smile I own, giving neither of them the slightest evidence of its haunting presence.

*** 

I open my eyes to see Mama lying on my old bed, her pale face turning toward me as I enter the pink walled room carrying a tray with steaming soup and hot tea.

"Hi, baby girl," she says hoarsely.

"Hi, Mama. Don't move. I'll help you."

Her limbs remain motionless, while her exhausted eyes trace my movements with delayed alertness. After setting the tray on the nightstand beside the bed, I lean across her frail figure to retrieve the extra pillow on the far side of the bed. I place the pillow on her chest for a moment before gently raising her to a sitting position. With a swift motion, I grasp the pillow on her chest and wedge it against the pillow behind her head. Propped up and looking relatively comfortable, Mama attempts to smile, but the movement of her bluish, chapped lips only strikes me as disturbing rather than comforting.

"Chicken noodle, my favorite," her raspy voice grinds against my ears.

"I know, Mama. That's why I've made it every day this week."

I observe the confusion lolling lazily across her expression. Resisting an irritated sigh, I instead raise the tray, extend the side flaps, and gingerly place the tray across her lap. Then I wait for her predictable response.

"*Every* day this week?" she asks, bewildered.

"Yes, every day, Mama. Now eat up. You have to see the doctor tomorrow and we need you to be at your best."

Her sagging frame heaves slightly. "I don't like the doctor."

"I know, Mama. I'm sure he doesn't like you either."

Now an ancient smile creeps across her lips. Her eyes dart with surprising quickness to my mine. "Thank you for the soup every day this week, baby."

I withhold another sigh and smile instead. "You're welcome, Mama. I'll be back to check on you in a little while."

I begin to head toward the open doorway, but I feel a tug at the bottom part of my shirt.

"Cindy."

Turning back around, I look at her oddly contented face.

"Yes, Mama?"

"I'm glad to be here in your old room. It has cheered me up, just as I hoped it would. Now I see why you always liked the pink walls. I hope you haven't minded sleeping upstairs."

"Not at all. If you want, I'll move down to the room next door on this floor, so I can watch over you better."

Her eyes glimmer with an eerie alarm. "No, baby, no. You *need* to stay up there. It would be best if you stayed up there as long as you live here."

She sees my confusion. "Why, Mama?"

"Because that's the way it needs to be. Grandma stayed in that room, then I stayed in that room, and now you will stay in that room. This place is yours now, so you must always take care of it and keep it as your own. There will be enough money for you never to work again. This is the family's house and it's your turn to watch over it. Do you understand?"

I allow the unnerving pause to settle in while gathering my thoughts. "I know I've only been here a couple of months without a job, but I plan to work again, Mama. I came to take care of you, but eventually I'm going back to work. I'm not locking myself in this house every day to do nothing but cook and clean. You aren't serious, are you?"

Her eyes are fixed in their fiery resolve, a firmness I have not seen since I was a teenager. "There is enough money, Cindy. Enough money for everything you need. Grandma gave us a fortune in her will, and all of it belongs to you now. She was not the kind of woman I want you to be, but she was good enough to provide us with all the money you will ever need so that you can become the kind of woman *I* want you to be."

Her final statement resonates in my mind as I stare at her pale, earnest face. I take a step back and survey the contrast between her ghastly figure and the bright pink wall behind her.

"What is it, baby?"

"Enjoy your soup, Mama."

As I reach the open doorway leading into the dark hallway beyond, I close my eyes.

I open my eyes to see Tony seated across from me on an armchair in the library. His eyes sparkle with anticipation. I clear my throat and exhale slowly.

"I was here, taking care of my mother. She told me about the money Grandma had left us."

He nods thoughtfully. "Did you remember anything else?"

I close my eyes briefly as the image of bloodied hands reaching for a bloodied knife imbedded in the pink wall flashes across my mind.

"No, nothing."

He stands up abruptly, targeting me with his outstretched finger. "There it is again."

"What?"

"That expression. The aversion reaction. You're seeing something, aren't you? Tell me what you're seeing."

I glance to the floor. "I'm hungry. Do you want something to eat?"

"Don't avoid me, Cindy."

"Or you could kiss me."

He arrives at the edge of my armchair and kneels down so our eyes are level.

"Please talk to me."

I surrender my gaze to his piercing stare. "I really am hungry. I don't remember anything else."

He rises to look down on me. "Fine. I'll go get us some lunch."

I grasp his arm tightly. "I can make food here."

He directs his eyes toward the center room. "I need to take a drive. I'll pick up something."

His sudden movement causes me to release his arm. I watch him exit the library and disappear around the corner.

*** 

*Mama, I have another question to ask you. This one is different than past inquiries about who I should date or how I know when I'm in love or why Daddy beat you.*

*I need to know, did I kill you? These images keep coming to me, of a bloody knife, and bloody hands, and you being gone already. Since I can't remember how you died, it makes me wonder.*

*Did I become fed up with taking care of you, did staying here remind me of everything I had tried to escape, did you lose your mind or did I lose mine? I know the answer waits in my memory, but I don't want to revisit that place for fear of what I will find. If you could simply tell me now, then I could have your version of it. Perhaps then the truth could be easier to avoid, or at least easier to revise so I can edit out the shame.*

*** 

Styrofoam containers holding half-eaten chicken salads rest on the kitchen countertop. I sit within arm's reach of the salads, awash in memories provoked by my feet dangling toward the floor.

Marlene talking to no one in particular about how the cabbage is calling out to be washed. Harold peeking his head in from the kitchen door to report on Grandma's fussy mood this morning. The sight of freshly cut cucumbers looking like mini Frisbees on the serving platter.

Then I snap back to attention at the sound of his voice. My focus redirects to Tony standing in the middle of the kitchen floor. He paces like a cat hunting a rodent.

"Does it have to do with the money or your mom's death in general?"

I sigh and scratch my fingers on the countertop. "I told you, all I saw was a bloody knife and a pair of bloody hands. They might not have even been my hands."

"You don't think that—"

"No, I didn't kill my mama, Tony. Are you kidding me?"

"I'm only trying to explore every possibility."

"Well, explore something else. It's not your responsibility to fix me. Can we just have a quiet afternoon and snuggle up on the couch or something?"

He shakes his head swiftly. "We need to do this before another episode sets in. Does it have to do with the garden or what used to be the gazebo or tool shed? By the way, whatever happened back there? Why's it so overgrown when the inside of this place is spotless? Or maybe it's the whole candle lighting routine you do every night."

"Let it go, Tony." .

He stops pacing and stares at me.

I return his stare without flinching. "I'm not your personal puzzle; I'm not solvable. I have to go at a slower pace because my mind is fragile right now. Please be sensitive to that. I realize you're trying to help, but this is the part where I need the man who cares about me, not the therapist who only cares about my issues. Okay?"

The intensity in his eyes does not lessen. "We need to find whatever is the trigger. It's the red room, isn't it?"

My eyes bulge, and I feel my face losing color. *Protect yourself, Cindy. He is trying to steal your secret. If he finds out what happened, he will leave you. Save him from causing you pain.*

"Get out."

"What?" His eyes become pitiful.

*The secret is more important than a relationship with him. Make him leave you alone.*

"I said get out. Get out of my house right now."

"Cindy, you asked me to help you. I'm doing what you asked."

"And now, I'm asking you to leave."

We look at each other for a moment. Then he turns and heads swiftly out of the kitchen.

Another moment passes before the image returns. A one-inch wide paint brush swiping a stroke against the wall, running like a river of red over the pink landscape beneath it.

"Tony, come back."

The front door opens and closes.

"Tony, come back."

The distant hum of a car engine, followed by tires scraping roughly against gravel, finds my ears.

"Come back," I whisper. The tremor in my right hand has already begun.

I grip my right hand with my left hand to hold it in place and lower myself off the countertop to a standing position. The spastic twitch runs up to the forearm and elbow joint of my right arm as I move toward the kitchen door.

"Come back. Please, come back." I hear myself whispering the words hoarsely.

After stumbling out of the kitchen and across the floor of the center room, I close my eyes to picture the red river slicing through the heart of the pink landscape. Then I force my eyes open, enter the library, and snatch up the phone from the end table to dial and apologize to his answering machine. I release my erratically shaking right arm and use my left hand to dial *CBT Guy*'s number, but the tingling numbness spreads through the fingers of both hands, causing me to lose my grip on the phone. The device slips out of my flailing grasp and plummets to the floor.

Unstable heaviness seeps into each joint and muscle, oozing down with terror to my waist, thighs, knees, and feet. My mind instructs my body to move in the direction of the front door, but the signal is swallowed in the ebb of syrupy, slow motion fatigue. My vision blurs indistinctly. The center of balance collapses as I topple out of the library and onto the edge of the center room floor.

The unforgiving wood greets my crumpled figure with bruising solitude. The sensation of paralysis conflicts with the rapid thrashing overtaking my limbs. Grunting, painful gasps spring up from my throat. Each breath burns, as I become desperate for disappearing air. The pressure in my head inflates, leaving the constricted oxygen to teeter my consciousness. Tears run down my face, stinging like needle pricks on my skin.

*You're going to die this time, Cindy. No one will save you. It's time to enter the darkness.*

*No, don't listen to her, Cindy. Breathe, you have to breathe. He'll come. He has to come.*

*He's gone. Just like everyone else in your life, he's gone. Soon you'll be gone too.*

*Please, Cindy, you must breathe.*

My vision fills with bloody hands holding a bloody knife stuck into a pink wall.

*You're going to lose consciousness and no one will find you. No one will miss you. You are completely alone.*

*He has to come. Keep breathing.*

The red river covers the pink landscape.

*You're going to die.*

*You have to breathe.*

*Give in, it's over.*

*You have to remember.*

*Fall into the abyss.*

*You have to remember to breathe.*

*It's time for you to die!*

*You have to breathe to remember!*

My vision opens to Mama lying on the small bed, her appearance looking ghostly against the cheery colored pink sheets. I am seated on the edge of the bed with bloodless hands and no knife in sight.

"You look thoughtful, baby." Her voice is wafer thin.

"More worried than deep in thought."

"I enjoyed the soup today. Was that chicken noodle?"

"Yes, Mama."

"I like chicken noodle. I can't remember the last time I've had it."

"Yesterday, Mama, and the day before."

"That's nice. Seems I'm having trouble with my memory. Glad you're here to take care of everything and remember the important things."

"Of course, Mama."

Her bluish, chapped lips smile. She looks away to the tall, oval mirror against the far wall. "Thought I'd live to see you become married and happy, but I guess I didn't give you a good example of how to be either one of those things. I'm sorry, baby."

"Mama, let's not talk about that right now—"

"Now is all I have, baby." Her eyes remain fixed on the mirror. "Your daddy loved you, but he also hated you, because you tied him to me, and he didn't want me no more. I'll never know why he took out his hate on me, why he forced his failure on me with his fists. There was nothing wrong with him, just nothing right with him. I'm sorry I chose that man, and I'm sorry he became your daddy."

I wait for her to turn her eyes to me, but she remains fixed in a trance, her attention fully absorbed by the mirror as if she can see something beyond her own reflection.

"I brought you here because I knew Grandma had money. She was as evil as your daddy in her own way, but she was rich and she was our way out. Now you have more money than you'll ever need, so you can be happy in ways I could never make possible for you. But now I know why you're sadder than I am. I wasn't the mama you needed. I set you up for a hard life, baby girl, and you didn't deserve that. I replaced your daddy with your grandma, and you didn't deserve that either. I'm sorry for being what you shouldn't have had in a mama. But maybe with this house and this money, you can have a life here that you really deserve."

At last her watery eyes turn to mine. My tears sting as they fall. I reach into my pocket and retrieve two small objects.

"I brought you something for old time's sake, Mama."

Her eyes light up and her lips find their way into a beautiful smile. "Really?"

"Really," I say, placing a Hershey's Kiss in her palm.

"One," I begin.

"Two," she replies.

"Three," we call in unison.

Her arthritic hands struggle to pry open the wrapper, but she manages the task without my assistance. We pop the treasures into our mouths and chew decadently.

"Still my favorite," Mama says, breathing a contented sigh.

"Mine too," I reply, gently stroking her clammy arm.

She giggles hoarsely. "Chocolate 'til the day I die."

Then she musters up her last remnants of strength, propping herself on her elbows and inching toward me.

"It is up to you to change our family, to start something new. I know you'll make me proud, as you always have."

I reach out and embrace her frail yet resilient figure one last time.

"I love you, Mama."

"I love you too, Cindy. Be better than me, baby. Be better than me."

*You have to breathe to remember.*

My vision opens to a gravestone surrounded by grass. The solitude of the graveyard hangs heavily in the air, a serene yet excruciating weight. A light mist dabs moisture onto my face, mixing with the thick tears cascading to the soggy earth below. With my hands shoved deep into my jacket pockets, I bite my lower lip and survey the gravestone, *Lisa James 1940-1985*. Fresh flowers picked from the backyard garden array the base of the stone. My eyes glance to the left to see Grandma's headstone, *Elaine James 1913-1976*. With a sigh, I move my eyes back to Mama's stone in front of me.

"I'll take care of everything, Mama. I promise."

*You have to breathe to remember.*

My vision opens to the pink walled room and an empty bed. Dry tear stains on my cheeks feel cold, nearly numb. I walk across the room, pass around the bed, and come to the tall, oval mirror. The face of the woman in the mirror appears lost. She stares at me the same way I stare at her, but we are seeing two different people. I am watching the child who had to become a woman before she was ready, and she is watching the woman who has no child left in her, only a weary solitude to share with herself in this massive, hollow house. As I picture her, I hate her, for she pities me. She has no sorrow for me, only spite disguised as sympathy. I must not allow her to see me anymore. She will only remind me of all that is gone, of all I wanted to be but now am not.

I reach to the top of the mirror and pull against the wooden frame. The nails pinning the mirror to the wall groan in resistance. Water wells within my eyes. With a forceful tearing motion, I jar the top portion of the mirror from the wall. After lowering my hands to either side of the wooden frame, I rip it from the wall, sending nails loose to bounce across the floor.

I toss the mirror onto the pink sheeted bed. Then I turn my gaze back to the space on the wall where the mirror had stood, my eyes widening in amazement. A hole roughly two feet tall and one foot across sits embedded in the dry wall. Waiting just beyond the opening of the hole is a rectangular wooden box I have seen before. I stretch my hands into the wall and withdraw the box containing Grandma's knives. In disgust, I lean over and discard the box next to the mirror on the bed. I move to leave the room, but something deeper within the wall cavity catches my eye.

I reach a hand against the dry wall edges and retrieve another rectangular wooden box. After brushing off the debris-covered lid, I open the box and sense the blood draining from my face. A carving knife covered with dried blood rests in the box. Attached to the knife is a picture of Daddy labeled *Dear Curtis Young*.

The box falls from my hands. The sound of the knife bouncing against the floor reminds me of the sound of the knife clanging against the kitchen floor on the day Mama stopped Daddy from hurting us. A shudder passes through my body. Guilt, then despair, then rage rises within me.

I kneel down, pick up the bloody knife, and hold it by the handle. Then I stand and look down at the mirror atop the pink sheeted bed. After one final glance, I slam the knife blade against the glass. A dull puncturing sound ricochets from the glass as a crack appears and webs out. My tears begin sprinkling across the glass as the knife strikes it again and again until it shatters. I stab the pink sheets on the bed, inserting the blade and then slicing downward to tear them beyond repair. Using my free hand, I hoist up the other closed wooden box and fling it against the wall, watching the two bloody carving knives jostle loose and land harmlessly on the floor at the base of the wall.

My breath escapes in labored gasps. Water runs freely down my face. I stare at the knife in my right hand and feel its pull. I glance to my left wrist and see the answer clearly. I grit my teeth and dig the knife into my wrist cross ways, watching the red river run down my forearm and begin dripping onto the floor. The pain is unfelt. I press the knife deeper into the flesh, screaming as the agony erupts in my veins.

After jarring the blade loose from my wrist, I watch the wound spurt with a rich red color that contrasts the pink walls around me. The liquid moves in a free current and waterfalls off my arm to pool on the floor below. I stare at the knife, seeing the newly wet blood mingle with the old, dried blood. Horror shakes my limbs with a pulsing shock. I cry out and step toward the wall, plunging the knife against the pink surface. I stab the wall repeatedly until my strength vanishes. Then I stick the knife into the wall and withdraw my quivering, bloody hands. After collapsing to the floor, I wait for long-awaited relief to run its course and release me.

*You have to breathe to remember.*

My eyes open groggily to see Tony's face looming overhead. His eyes swell with panic. "Hold on, Cindy!"

*You have to breathe to remember.*

I look up to see flashing fluorescent lights lining the ceiling of a white corridor.

*You have to breathe to remember.*

A glimpse of Dr. Shipper's concerned face fills my vision.

*You have to breathe to remember.*

Terror-stricken faces crowd around, wet with tears. Tony, Jody, Samantha. Their faces become blurry. The image dissipates.

*You have to breathe to remember.*

## *Chapter Twenty*

The warmth of bed sheets enfolds my body. I sense the sunlight before seeing it. The air resting against my face seems lighter, broken of its oppressive weight. I find myself eager to open my eyes and face this new day, which is why I know this must be a dream.

My eyelids flutter and widen to allow sight. Tony, Jody, and Samantha sit on dining room chairs at the edge of my bed, waiting with expressions of eternal patience. My eyes roam their faces, not awake enough to be nervous yet.

"It's about time you woke up," Jody says, folding her arms.

"What happened to me?"

Jody smiles grimly. "You were hospitalized for three days, honey. Now you're home, and you've been asleep for hours. You don't remember anything?"

"No, nothing."

Tony chuckles. "I doubt that."

Samantha leans forward in her chair. "What were you thinking, Cindy?"

"I don't know what you mean. What's going on?"

Jody reaches below her chair and raises a slew of sample pill packets. "I told you to be careful with this crap. Were you *trying* to kill yourself? Just be glad the violent seizure was the worst thing that happened to you. If Tony hadn't come back to find you, we'd be gathered around a tombstone instead of your bed."

My eyes dare to meet Tony's. He glowers at me with angered pain.

"I'm sorry," I say shakily.

He glances at the floor. "I'm sure you are. I guess you were a better liar than I thought, making me believe you had thrown those pills away. Don't make me regret feeling bad for storming out and then deciding to come back and apologize."

Jody stirs with agitation, shaking the packets vigorously. "If you weren't my best friend, I'd beat you senseless. You knew these were dangerous. I gave them to you to help you, not so you could hurt yourself. I thought you had more sense than that; I thought you'd learned from before. Does that scar on your wrist mean anything to you? Don't you think I've had enough recurring nightmares about walking in to find you bleeding to death? Why didn't you talk to us?"

My eyes plead. "I did."

"Stop lying to yourself, Cindy," Samantha interjects.

Jody tosses the pill packets onto the floor. "Agreed. Now, something happened ten years ago after I found you. You were in the hospital for a few weeks, recovering, and then you went home and pushed Samantha and me away for the rest of the summer. I remember you coming out several months later, acting fine, ready to open your therapy practice and seeming perfect. You fooled us into believing you had fixed yourself. But I know something happened to change you and you hid it from us. Now you're going to tell us what it was."

I look at their faces and expel a lengthy sigh. Then I glimpse the scar across my left wrist before closing my eyes to reenter the darkness.

My bloodshot eyes shoot open to the weed-riddled garden in the backyard of the house. The refreshing scent of flowers has been constricted by wild, untended greenery. The manicured flower beds have been reduced to piles of strewn dirt, soggy with rain, blown out of their old boundaries by wicked winds.

I clench my fists at the sight of the yard's corruption and feel something within me snap, a final punishing straw on the back of my beaten sanity. Within moments, I am tearing into and then out of the tool shed, hefting a sledgehammer.

The gazebo is my first target, a fragile structure I hack to pieces with vicious swings and sweat. Next I work my way to the rod iron archways, which collapse easily after the bulky head of the hammer strikes them without warning. I glance at the tool shed, determining to come back later to finish it off. Brisk steps around the side of the house to the driveway lead me to the large stone plant pots, which are promptly destroyed.

My tears and my sweat become indistinguishable, forming a collective mat of sticky filth on my burning face. I wield my instrument of wreckage inside, pounding the wretched goddess statues until they are nearly powder, purging the reminder of Grandma's image with each jubilant, frenzied whack. Every muscle screams for relief, every joint howls its threats of pain to plague me in the days to come.

After tossing the tool of torture aside, I scurry from room to room, upending furniture, scratching priceless antiques, shattering mirrors large and small. I pitch chairs and jewelry and lamps and bed sheets and books and clocks and clothes over the banisters, watching them with glee as they meet their hardwood demise.

I make special efforts in the pink room, ripping out the bookcase and clothes rack, shredding the childhood garments, and puncturing the glass window. Still empowered by my self-control-less streak, I race around the house to gather a regular hammer, nails, a one-inch-wide brush, and two cans of paint hidden in the back of the kitchen pantry which have been awaiting use for an entire year. Then I return to the hideous pink room.

For the next several minutes, I board up the broken window, sealing it shut from the outside world forever.

For the next several hours, I paint the room red, inch by inch, moving ever so slowly, soaking up every corner, every crevice, every minute particle of its surface. Then I paint it again. Then I paint it again.

After taking a brief break to wash my face and wrap Band-Aids around my blistered and bloodied fingers, I haul two more buckets of paint from the kitchen pantry up to the red room.

Then I paint it again. Then I paint it again. Then I paint it again.

When the sixth coat is complete, I blink and the red room disappears.

I blink and Tony's face reappears.

I swallow hard and shiver. His eyes are no longer condemning; instead, they are compassionate. I look to Jody and Samantha, seeing the same concern covering their faces.

"I lost my mind," I begin softly. "I wrecked the house and tried to erase all the memories I had in this place. I even gave away Grandma's Cadillac and Daddy's beat up truck. I planned to kill myself every day, but I kept hearing Mama's voice in my head, telling me it was my time to take care of the house, so I kept waking up and living. I beat myself into this house and felt it being beaten into me. I began chronically cleaning during the day like Mama had, and I started lighting candles at night like Grandma did. I always hoped one of the candles would tip over and the fire could consume everything and take me with it."

I inhale a deep breath and release it, sensing the tears rising. I stare at the scar on my wrist, allowing it to blur in my watery sight.

"I hated myself, I hated who I had become in this place, but I knew I couldn't leave. I had to keep myself alive to make sure the house stayed alive, and the only way to do that was to prove to everyone I was all right by becoming perfect. And the more I perfected myself, the more I pushed back the memories of what happened, until I no longer believed them at all. That was another person, not me; that was someone else's tragic, miss-lived life, not mine."

I look up to absorb their reactions. Tony stands and shoves his hands into his blue jean pockets. His eyes rove to the far wall.

"Why did you start taking the pills again?"

"I don't know."

"Did you plan to kill yourself?"

"No."

"Did you plan to hurt yourself?"

"No."

"Did you want one of us to find you?"

"No, what the—"

"Was this your way of calling out for help?"

"No! Shut up and listen to me!"

He turns his head in my direction and glares at me. The compassion of moments ago has vanished from his eyes, replaced by a startling sternness. "I'm just trying to understand why you've brought yourself back to the same place you were—willing to end your life."

"I don't have any answers for you, Tony. Obviously, I'm broken beyond repair."

"I didn't say that—"

"That's what you meant!" I growl, feeling my insides boil.

*Push him away, Cindy. He's dangerous. You don't want him anymore.*

"Please go away," I say, nearly breathless.

"Are you serious?" he asks, incredulous. "After all this, you want me gone?"

*Send him out of your life. We don't need him.*

The tears fall freely. "I don't know why you're sticking around. It's not a beautiful thing you're going to find when you reach the end of me. You're better off without the burden of a damaged woman. You say you love me, but all you want to do is fix me. I've been fine for years and I'll continue being fine. You're free to leave."

Jody squirms uneasily in her chair. "Now, wait a minute—"

"It's fine," Tony interjects, holding up his hands in absolution. His voice is heavy with feeling. "I do love you, Cindy, and there is nothing in you to be fixed, only something to be found. You deserve a better life, even if you don't want it."

He turns and steps through the open doorway. His quick, choppy footsteps ricochet off the walls around the levels. Jody, Samantha, and I sit in silence, not daring to make eye contact.

*** 

*Mama, I wish you had taught me how to live, rather than only teaching me how to escape life. I know you wanted better for me, but you never showed me what that was or how to find it. You taught me to be discontent with myself and unsettled in the choices I had made, because that's what I always saw in you. How I've craved your advice and your support through these dark years, but you never chose to have enough light in you to reach out to me and walk me though this life. I wish I was half the woman you were, and yet I want to be twice the woman you could not bring yourself to be.*

*Perhaps it wasn't weakness that crippled you, maybe it was only fear. Regardless, reimagining myself with love, strength, and the safety of support is too great a risk. I can only learn to take the best of what you gave me and hope to pick up the rest of what I need along the way. Yet the way ahead is shrouded by a fog of memories, the same burdens and terrors that have consumed my entire life. I can't move on; I can't move at all. It truly must be time to climb the banister and fall into the end of it.*

***

I awaken covered in sweat, struggling to catch my breath. After groping around, I feel Raggedy Ann close by. The creaks and groans of the house creep into my ears. The shadows on the ceiling created by the flickering candle light slither eerily back and forth in my vision. The presence of the house presses upon me with suffocating constriction.

Suddenly, a ringing sounds from the nightstand. Fumbling around, I pick up the phone and hold my breath.

"I forgive you," *CBT Guy*'s voice says plainly.

"I don't think you should."

"That's for me to decide."

"I'm not apologizing. I meant what I said. Didn't it hurt you to hear it?"

"Probably not as much as it hurt you to say it. So I forgive you."

I sigh heavily. "I don't want to be forgiven. Why would you assume I want to be with you?"

"Because you need someone equally broken to be a perfect match for you. I'm done trying to figure you out. I'm simply content to be with you, whether you want me or not."

Another heavy sigh. "I'm tired, Tony. I'm tired of myself. That's why I started taking the pills. I need relief from me. It's not about fixing a stress disorder or achieving some psychological breakthrough to stop my compulsive behaviors. I want to get away from me, and I'll try anything to do it."

"Is that what you really want? Or is that just another way of avoiding what you need?"

I bite my lip and wallow in a lingering pause. "I need to move on."

"How do you suppose you're going to do that?"

"I'll just let go and leave."

A hesitant pause fills the phone. "What do you mean by let go?"

"It means what I need it to mean."

He speaks with marked deliberation. "If you want real freedom, you have to earn it the hard way. But you already know that."

"I don't want your forgiveness."

The phone is silent for a few more moments. "It doesn't matter. You already have it. There's only one way to make this right. You know what you have to do, Cindy. You've known since you were thirteen."

Click.

\*\*\*

A faint knock echoes from the cherry wood door, bouncing off the red walls and into my waiting ears.

"Come in," I say quietly.

The door opens slowly and Tony steps into the room, surveying the scene with caution. I sit Indian-style in the center of the room. A carving knife stained with dried blood lies at a sideways angle, resting against my left wrist. Methodically, my right hand raises and lowers the knife so the blade slaps against my pale skin in rhythm.

"I came as soon as I got your message. Looks like you're having a good time," he comments, moving uneasily toward me, trying to maintain a casual expression.

"I needed to see you first before I let go," I whisper, my eyes delving into his.

Upon coming within arm's reach of me, he gently kneels down and sits Indian-style in front of me, mirroring my posture. His eyes glance warily to the knife blade rising and falling against the jagged scar on my left wrist.

He smiles nervously. "So, what's on your mind?"

"I've been remembering," I answer distantly.

His eyes dart to the knife and then back to my face. "Anything in particular?"

My eyes drift to the red wall behind him. "I've been remembering the last time I was in this room with this knife."

His jaw clenches anxiously. "Do you want to talk to me about it? I'm here, I'm listening."

My upper teeth grind against my lower lip. I lay the blade flat on my arm and expel a weighty sigh. Water stings my eyes.

"Do I have a purpose?"

His figure leans forward instinctively, but he restrains himself from reaching out to pry the knife away from my white-knuckled grip.

"Don't ask me that. Of course you have purpose."

My eyes plead with him. "What is it? What's the meaning of me?"

His eyes attempt to relax me, but his forced nonchalance only ignites my disturbance. My limbs begin trembling. His expression appears conflicted, unsure of how to proceed.

"If you don't know, I can't tell you."

"Why not?"

"Because you'll never believe me."

My jittery hand fastens its grasp on the knife handle. "But why am I still here? Why am I waking up, walking around, faking life, and lying my head down at night, dreading the realization that tomorrow brings only the same purposeless existence? What am I still doing alive?"

The knife blade turns gradually, touching the slicing edge tenderly against my wrist skin. His eyes widen and he swallows hard.

"Cindy, honey, you're still alive because you are too strong to end it. I don't see you as unstable or unloved or purposeless. You are simply hurting, hiding in the pain, losing yourself in the same memories you've been trying to block out for your entire life."

Tears begin cascading down my burning cheeks. "I just live, but I don't have a life. What's my purpose?" The tone in my voice intensifies with desperation. "Why shouldn't I end it? What's my purpose?"

He extends an unsteady hand and eases it onto the top of the knife blade. Our eyes remain locked.

"Your purpose is to live."

I grit my teeth as the gushing water blurs my vision. "I can't anymore. Look at me. Look at my family's legacy. I have no hope of changing. I've spent my life trying to give hope to others, but I have none for myself. There's no impact, no difference I've made. All of my life is wrapped up in this bloody knife. With a slip of the blade, I could be free. Don't you want me to be free?"

His shaking fingers pinch the blade and carefully draw it away from my wrist.

"Yes, I want you to be free, but not this way. This is only another escape, another gravestone."

Then he lowers the blade tightly against his own wrist. "If you're going to cut someone, cut me."

My hand stays firmly wrapped around the knife handle, while my eyes search his in anguish. "No, I can't."

His expression darkens, emboldened. "Do it, Cindy. I need you to. Cut me. Cut me!"

"I won't—"

"Cut me now!" He places his free hand onto the knife blade and pushes downward.

My body quakes, overwhelmed. "No!"

His torso surges forward until our faces are only inches apart. He stares into my eyes, agonized and panicked. "End it!"

"No, I won't!"

I swat away his pressuring hand, release the blade from his wrist, and hurl the carving knife against the wall. The stainless steel slams against the red landscape and careens to the floor. My trembling hand lashes out and strikes him across the cheek. His body stiffens. I lunge into him, collide with his solid form, and wrap my arms around his shoulders. Then I burrow my face into his neck and weep with sobs so forceful my breathing becomes strained and my body heaves.

After a few moments, his sweating hands cradle my face, lifting me so our eyes are level. His fingers brush away newly gathering tears from my eyelids.

My voice comes out in a faint whisper. "Why did you tell me to cut you?"

He smiles sadly. "So you could know how it feels for all of us who love you. You think nobody sees and nobody cares, no one would miss you, but if you truly believed that, then you would have cut me. You would have cut yourself and ended it long before I walked into this room. You've been crying out for help, trying to find meaning, but the purpose you keep missing is already in you."

I lean my forehead against his and shut my eyes tightly. "I can't see it. There's nothing but shadows and terrible memories. I can't leave; it won't leave me. It's impossible."

He sighs, his breath seeping onto my face with a fervent rush. "You have to let go. The only way to move on is to forgive. You've got to forgive them."

My body shudders and my fists clench. "They took away my life."

He pulls me closer, his lips finding my mouth in a gentle, trembling kiss. Then he releases me and looks decisively into my eyes.

"Then you take it back. You forgive and move on. You choose to live. You stop dying from the past and start living for your future. You need this. You need your own life. That's where your purpose is."

I unclench my fists and grip tightly to his shoulders for support. "All I have is pain."

Water drips from his eyes. "Then we heal." He clutches me to his chest and we remain motionless in an unwavering embrace. "Then we heal."

# *Chapter Twenty-One*

The densely humid September air lays stagnant across the interior of the house. Isolated rays of sunshine filter in through the narrow archway windows above the front double doors. Tony and I lay side by side in the middle of the center room floor, gazing up at the massive void between the levels. Our inside arms are cushioned against each other and our inside hands are interlocked. The unforgiving hardwood beneath us remains unfelt as we continue looking upward into the abyss, our heads resting close enough to touch one another.

"I crushed the pills Jody gave me and flushed them down the toilet," I say, hearing my voice swallowed into the thick atmosphere.

"I know. I was there."

"Just making sure it was real and not a dream."

We absorb the static silence for a minute, remaining motionless as we have for the past hour. Then the sound of him pursing his lips thoughtfully enters my ears.

"Do you think we can last together?" he asks.

I listen to the words hanging like a fog over us. My mind waits for a cautionary voice to rise from within, but only the lingering presence of his question occupies my thoughts. I close my eyes tightly, readying myself to wince, but then I open my eyes and hear myself uttering the words, "I need us to last."

His hand intertwining my hand squeezes tenderly. "We will—if you will."

I sense the security of his touch and exhale. "I don't need this in order to feel normal; I need it so I can feel life is possible, a life I never had the chance to have."

He allows the suspended pause to loll lazily across us. "So do you want to leave this place?"

I smile grimly, eyeing his stoic expression in my peripheral vision. "I've wanted to leave since the first day I set foot in this house. But being ready to leave, that is something altogether different. My life is tied up here, knotted in ways I don't know how to undo."

I stare into the void, suddenly fearing it will collapse upon my helpless figure and send me spiraling into forgotten nothingness. My eyes shut and I anxiously wait for the trembling in my limbs to begin. Suddenly, his offbeat voice startles me, causing my eyes to snap open to attention.

"My father was a strong man. He had the ability to read people in ways I will never match. He was patient, understanding, and the best therapist I've ever known. He had a peculiar hobby of collecting various types of rope. Thick ropes, thin ropes, long ropes, short ropes; it didn't matter, as long as it was a rope. He amassed a garage full of ropes and would spend weekends tying them together and making bizarre designs and shapes out of them. One day, I asked him why he had such an odd hobby and he told me the ropes reminded him of people—their memories, feelings, dreams, hopes, and pains, all intertwined. He explained to me that tying the ropes together helped him understand the complexities of people's lives and relationships."

He grows silent for a moment, as if traveling further into a memory.

"When I became a therapist myself, I often visited him in his garage on the weekends and we'd tie ropes together while catching up. I remember one particular visit where I was struggling with several different knotted ropes that wouldn't unwind and fit together. Using a single cord, I was trying to connect the knotted bundle to the rest of the cohesive design he was making. I gave up and handed my mess to him. He wrestled with the bundled ropes for a while and finally grabbed a carpet knife and cut the connective cord between my mess and his masterpiece. I was surprised and asked him why he had done it. He looked me squarely in the eyes, grinned, and said, 'Sometimes you need to sever what's holding you back from what you want to make of yourself.'"

He pauses, as if reliving the moment with perfect clarity. Then he breathes deeply.

"He died a year later, and when I was cleaning out his garage, I piled all the ropes I could find into a large box that I took home with me. Sometimes I rummage through my storage closet and open the box, just to see the ropes and to remember him. At the top of the box, the bundled rope mess I made sits next to his beautiful design. I think of what he said to me and of how he cut the cord that day. I keep my knotted bundle as a reminder of what I chose to let go. It makes the masterpiece next to it look even more rewarding."

A few moments pass before I release his hand, turn to lie on my side, and look at him. He adjusts his posture to face me, his eyes intensely focused.

"Tony, I have no example of how a good relationship should be. I know I love you and I know I want to leave, but how those things will actually work out is a mystery to me. If I leave, you need to leave with me, and if I break down and relapse into self-destructive thought patterns and behaviors, I need you to have the patience and understanding to carry me through those times. I'm sure I will need to see a psychiatrist to continue working through my issues. Life with me will probably never be easy, but I promise I will be honest with you. I will be loyal for life, and you know I don't say that lightly. Being alone has kept me chained to this place, and the only way I can sever myself from here and move on is to know I will not be alone when I leave."

He leans over to embrace and kiss me. Then he pulls away and fastens his stable gaze on my eyes. "I'm ready when you are."

I look at him intently, absorbing his understanding expression. "I'm meeting the girls at the diner for the last time to explain everything. I think they'll be glad I'm donating my practice to a women's shelter. I also have to go by the bank to close the accounts and visit the insurance office to iron out some final details. I'll pick up cleaning solution for the house so I can leave it in good order tonight."

He nods. "Whatever you need to do to move on."

"Will you say good-bye to Dr. Shipper for me when you meet him for lunch?"

He smiles. "Of course. I'm sure he will be happy not to see you anymore."

A calming silence occupies the space between us. We lay back and gaze into the void, sensing the significance of the moment. Then we rise from the floor and head in separate directions.

# *Chapter Twenty-Two*

My blue Ford Taurus winds along the gravel driveway, creeping slowly as if deep in thought. Large circular outlines in the earth on either side of the path serve as fading connections of memory to the ornate stone plant pots that once stood as awe-inspiring monuments leading to the estate beyond. I am remembering the first time I set eyes on this driveway, as Daddy's rusty truck carried Mama, me, and our garbage bag of possessions to our new home. Billowing tree branches overhung the gravel on that day, reaching down with embracing invitation. Now the trees are trimmed back and decaying, wearing the scars of the years upon them. That first day was marked by sunshine cascading through the tree line to light the road ahead. Now only the darkness of a muggy night greets my roving eyes.

I navigate the vehicle past the empty, crumbling water fountain. After pulling the car into the circle drive and turning off the engine, I pull out the keys and place them in my coat pocket. With soft steps onto the gravel, I move out of the car and close the door behind me. I head to the front double doors, unlock them, and quietly move inside to the library, where I deposit my purse, coat, and keys on top of the desk.

Then I turn and make my way back to the trunk of the car. My eyes rove to the driveway and I picture a young girl viewing the backyard garden for the first time, absorbing the array of multi-colored flowers and exotic scents. While shaking the image from my mind, I pop open the trunk and retrieve a short-handled mop and two five-gallon sealed buckets labeled *Floor Cleaning Solution*. After closing the trunk gently, I haul the buckets and mop to the middle of the center room floor, while sweat forms on my forehead.

My eyes sweep across the room to the front entry door. In my memory, I envision a wide-eyed girl beaming at the sight of offsetting stone statues of goddess-looking women looming as threshold guardians. The massive center room fills up her view, enchanting her imagination with its shiny wooden floors, its rooms spread throughout with hidden secrets to be discovered, and its gaping cavity of space leading up to heaven. Now I look at the same room from my perspective and see only remnants of the square pedestals on which the statues once stood. The floor does not sparkle but remains washed in shadows, and the towering cavern overhead serves as nothing more than a blank space leading nowhere but back to the bottom where I stand.

I glance at the two buckets and sigh, sensing the sting of water burning in my eyes.

*You can do this, Cindy, one last time. Leave it clean. Leave it clean.*

My hands grip a bucket handle and the mop and I lift them to my side. The dark interior swarms around me as I move toward the stairs. Faint traces of moonlight trickle in through the front entrance archway windows. The house is disturbingly still, silent in echoless solitude.

While lugging the bucket and mop up the stairs to the second level, I imagine the young girl eating lasagna, smearing sauce across her mouth with each ravenous bite. I ascend to the third level. I see the girl opening the pink wrapped box to find a whole-headed Raggedy Ann. My feet take me up to the fourth level. An image flashes of the girl being walked out of the room by the grandma goddess, while Mama's empty eyes stare at the table. The fifth level arrives. I picture the girl's eyes marveling at her new bedroom and the tall, oval mirror, wondering how such a beautiful place could be her home.

I set down the bucket and mop, observing the darkness of the interior lying particularly prevalent on the top level. With a careful motion, I lean over and undo the bucket lid. A strong scent rushes into my nostrils, but I do not turn my head away. I lace my fingers around the mop, raise the cotton fabric end, and lower it gingerly into the solution. Liquid sloshes around in the bucket. After feeling the mop increase in weight from the saturated end, I pull the mop out of the bucket and place it on the floor. I turn around and begin mopping the hallway in a backward motion.

The whooshing sound of liquid-drenched cloth rubbing against the wooden floor is the only noise reverberating in my ears.

I progress backward, feeling my way in memory down the hallway behind me, sweeping the mop in even, calculated strokes back and forth. I arrive at the first room on the side wall. The door is already open, so I move inside and mop the floor from end to end. Then I proceed back into the hallway and continue my circuit. Upon coming to my open bedroom doorway, I pause and look into the dark room for a moment. Then I turn away from the doorway and continue mopping across the hallway.

The next hour passes in precise sequence as I clean the hallways and room floors on the fifth, fourth, and third levels, making sure the window curtains are closed in each room. As planned, the cleaning solution from the first bucket runs out as I reach the red room. After leaning the mop against the door, I pick up the empty bucket, descend to the center room, switch out the buckets, and haul the second batch of cleaning solution up to the third level. Then I plunge the mop into the new solution and pick up where I left off, while leaving the red room door unopened. After mopping across the hallway to the set of stairs, I raise the bucket and descend to the second level.

Another hour ticks by slowly as I complete the hallways and rooms of the second level, as well as the kitchen, dining room, and library on the first floor. Then I sweep the mop in perfect patterns across the center room floor until the cleaning solution bucket lies empty with the final strokes in front of the entryway doors. After laying the mop onto the bucket top, I lean against the wall and gaze into the dark house. Sweat drenches my shirt and frizzes my hair. The overpowering scent of the cleaning solution is slightly nauseating. I imagine the disarray of my makeup due to the sweat-smeared tears glistening on my cheeks.

I sigh deeply and close my eyes, picturing Mama standing over Daddy in the kitchen, holding a bloody knife. The wild look in her eyes calls out to me, wanting me to feel her rage, her terrified pain. She stares at me with those anguished eyes, capturing the sadness of a thousand abuses and a million regrets. I see her and I understand her, but I know I cannot be the girl she knew before that day. We watch each other, knowing everything changed in that moment. She never had a chance to climb Lookout Mountain with me and stare up at the stars, feeling like our horrible life could be forgotten for just one night. We never shared the moments we were supposed to have together: her taking proud pictures of me with some awkwardly handsome boy before going to prom; her helping me put on my wedding dress before I walked down the aisle; her holding my hand and telling me she loved me and was proud of me as I brought her granddaughter into the world. We never had the chance to have these memories, and it is these memories taken away from us before they could ever happen that I miss as much as the memories I actually had with her.

Yet, as I imagine her looking at me in the kitchen on the day everything changed, I sense her eyes telling me I can move on now; I can let her go because she will remain with me. Someday, we will sit with one another and share stories over a bowl of non-generic Corn Flakes, without tears, without purple bruises, and without bloodied noses. That is how I will see Mama now—as whole and strong. This is how I will remember her.

My mind flashes to my reflection in the tall, oval mirror in my pink bedroom. I look for the ghostly features, I wait for the little girl clutching the headless Raggedy Ann doll, but all I see is myself. The face in me stares at me, unchanging. There is something in those eyes: a fire and the courage to have a new vision of me. More than mere confidence, those eyes speak with meaning I have never heard before. They see a purpose in me. They tell me I am worth looking at. They assure me that I can walk away and walk on because I am like Mama, whole and strong. As I watch myself, I witness the tears falling from my eyes and the smile rising to grace my mouth.

I open my eyes to see the dark house waiting before me. My feet stand firmly on the freshly washed floor, allowing the moisture to soak up into my shoe soles. Following a quick glance down at my watch in the moonlight, I hastily retrieve the empty buckets and mop and scurry outside. After popping the car trunk open once more, I deposit the items into the trunk bed.

Then I venture back past the center room and head upstairs to my bedroom. I come to my doorway and step inside, sensing an unusual calm resting over the room. I glance around to ensure the exact location of my belongings as I placed them this morning. A powerful presence feels tangible in the room. I wipe my eyes and creep over to the bed to find a wrinkled picture of Mama and me in my pink walled room. Next to the familiar picture is a smaller, less familiar picture, a picture of Daddy labeled *Dear Curtis Young.* The pictures edges are touching, leaving me between the two of them.

"Hi, Mama and Daddy," I whisper. "I've always loved you because you were my parents, but I hated you because of the life you gave me. I'm done hating you now. I'm moving on to remember you only with love, because I forgive you. The pain has taken up too much of who I am already. So I let go of all I needed that you never gave to me, and I hold onto the love that we wanted to share but somehow lost between us. I want to be free. I have a life to live, so I love you, good-bye."

Without another word, I grasp the pictures and shove them deeply into my pocket. Arriving at the nightstand, I slide open the top drawer and retrieve the long-nosed lighter. With a deep breath of reassurance, I fetch a single candle nestled in the back of the same drawer. Then I leave my room for the last time.

I quickly descend to the third floor, hastening to the red room. Upon prying open the door, I step inside and squint to make out headless Raggedy Ann lying in the center of the floor. Using the lighter, I add a flame to the wick of the candle in my hand. The room glows amid flickering shadows. My feet inch me closer until I arrive in the center of the room beside the decapitated doll. I sit on the floor, place the candle and lighter to the side, and close my eyes.

My memory flashes with the image of a young girl hiding beneath her bed, clutching a Raggedy Ann who has a whole head. A piece of pink wrapping paper reading *Happy 9$^{th}$ Birthday, Cindy!* is still taped to a Goodwill sticker fastened to the front of the doll. The girl stares at the paper but struggles to focus on the words it says because of the terrible sounds coming from the kitchen. She cannot hold the doll and cover her own ears at the same time, so the girl begins to cry. Then she says, "I'm sorry," to Raggedy Ann and rips her head off so the poor doll will not have to see or hear anymore. The frightened girl takes the doll's smiling head and buries it in the cockroach-infested corner of the wall below her bed, not realizing that the next time she crawls under the bed to find it, the head will be hollowed out and nibbled to death by the mice living in the wall. The girl does her best to pin the doll against her stomach by using her elbows, while she shields her ears with her cupped hands. Her tears drip down painfully to wet the floor and splash against the backs of the cockroaches.

I open my eyes and stare down at headless Raggedy Ann. After a moment, I pick her up and hold her to my chest. We look at the floor, as the scent of cleaning solution from outside drifts into the room, causing my head to swirl with dizziness. I place Raggedy Ann back onto the floor, look at my watch, and reach down to unlace my shoes and remove my socks. Within moments, I stand up on bare feet and stuff my socks into my shoes. Then I lay the shoes close together on their sides, with the soles facing inward. I lift Raggedy Ann and lay her to rest on top of the shoes.

"Thank you, good-bye," I whisper.

She answers with silence.

My trembling hand grips the lit candle beside me and moves it to touch the doll. I watch as the flame crawls onto her, consuming the fabric skin of her torso and extending to her arms and legs. After a final, long gaze at the funeral pyre, I extinguish the candle with my breath and place it on the floor. Then I rise to look around at the red walls. I reach out to touch one of the walls, feeling the memory fog swelling within me. My eyes dart back to the fire consuming my precious doll, which has now grazed my shoe soles. The second the flame touches the gasoline cleaning solution oozing from the bottom of my shoes, it causes a forceful fire to erupt instantly. The blaze begins to lick the wooden floor below.

Turning away, I walk out of the red room and across the hallway, feeling the gasoline slathered across the wooden floor squish between my toes. After descending the staircase to the bottom level, I move to the middle of the center room and take in the view. The smell of gasoline, fire, and smoke filters into my nostrils. I watch the flames filling the red room above.

Suddenly, the fire, which has reached as far as the hallway, greets the gasoline with a swelling inferno. The orange glow ignites with whooshing force and barrels down either side of the hallway. The wooden banisters, walls, and floors are lapped up in flame within moments.

I offer a simple smile and then I look away from the devastation and head toward the front double doors. I find myself stepping out of the house and walking with light-footed ease onto the circle drive. A weathered Pontiac Grand Am, still dirty, without headlights shining, waits in front of the water fountain. I tiptoe to the car, gently open the door, slide into the passenger seat, and close the door. Tony looks at me plainly, acknowledging the resolve in my eyes.

"You okay?"

"I will be," I answer softly.

The car circles around the water fountain and moves quietly away from the massive house, which is now engulfed in flames that are spreading from the interior to the outer walls. We weave along the gravel path until coming to the road. The vehicle stops momentarily.

"Where to now?" he asks, placing a calming hand on my trembling hand.

"I want to go home," I whisper, feeling my breath catch.

I sense him gazing at me intently. "And where is home?"

I glance over to him and smile. "Wherever we are."

He nods, gives my hand a squeeze, and turns the vehicle left onto the road, heading toward the highway that leads out of Sleepy Oak. As we round the corner, I glance back in the rear window to see towering flames and billowing smoke rising above the tree line. Then I turn around and fix my eyes forward, remembering not to look back.

# *Chapter Twenty-Three*

*Mama, I've been remembering you, and that finally comforts me. The health episodes have ceased at last. I have the new beginning I have needed since the day we first climbed into the truck and left Daddy.*

*I hope you can forgive me for the things I've done, just as I've forgiven you. This life of mine doesn't fit together perfectly, but at least it fits somewhere now. I've finally come to see some beauty and purpose in the pain, a flicker of hope. I just wish you were here with me to see it too.*

*I know you would be upset that I burned the money, all of it. I closed the account, piled the bills under the bed on top of the three carving knives, and let everything be consumed with the rest of the house. You would think me foolish for canceling the house insurance, but I didn't want a penny of blood money from that giant prison once I decided to destroy it. Setting the house on fire is something I don't expect you to understand, but I only ask that you accept my decision not to tie up my future in the past of that place.*

*I come from a line of strong-willed women who bottle up the pain until it finds its voice at the striking end of a knife, but I hope that cycle stops with me. I want to change our family legacy and rewrite the script that was set in motion for me to follow. I'm not sure if you'd be proud of me, I'm not sure if you'd be disappointed in me, but I am sure you'd love me as I am, and for that reason I will always remember you as a strong woman. Now I'll have the chance to be that for someone else.*

*Love you, and I'll write again soon.*

I set the journal pad and pen on the cherry wood end table. The sturdy rocking chair beneath me offers solid support as I gently lean in soothing rhythm. My left hand, clad with a silver ring, reaches down to my protruding belly, placing my open palm against the warm surface where a kick occurred only moments ago.

"So, now you know, baby," I whisper, hoping you will receive my tone as something of sweetness to savor. "Someday I'll tell you the story again—a revised version, of course—in a way that you can understand it. But for now, I want you to know how important it is for me to do this, to keep telling it, to keep remembering it. I want you to know it now, so when I tell it to you later, you'll remember and still stay with me. Something new starts with you, and I will never stop speaking with you, I will never stop being with you."

I steady myself and rise from the rocking chair. After a few laborious steps, I stop in front of a sparkling tall, oval mirror. As I stare at myself and the swollen bump attached to me, a smile forms on my lips and tears glisten in my eyes. I breathe a full, refreshing breath, sensing your tiny foot kicking me from within once again.

"Be better than me, baby," I say, my eyes fixed on your reflection in the mirror. "Be better than me."

My eyes move in the mirror from the swollen bump up to the face of the woman looking back at me. I recognize this face, this person, this me. She was only missing after all, never non-existent. There is something worth watching in her eyes: life and purpose. I know her; she has been looking for me everywhere, and I've finally been found. Now she is here, she is with me, and I will not forget her.

I glance over to notice Grandma's ancient marble chess set perched upon an end table surrounded by two chairs in the far corner of the room. As I glimpse the chess pieces, I recall myself not being able to destroy this "distinct character" item of Grandma's collection because it was the only object about which I had good memories. A smile finds my lips. Just like the chess set, I only want to remember the good from now on.

Then I fix my eyes on the mirror again, feeling your tiny foot nudging me once more, bringing a ripple of connection between us. Resolve rises in me as I observe our reflection. I refuse to pass on to you the poison that was passed on to me; I must show you a different way to live. I am responsible for you, a life springing from both my body and from my deepest person. The cords of my legacy will be transferred to you, and now I have to choose every day what that legacy will be. My greatest fear was to become like my mama, and now I want to live in such a way so you will not have that same fear for yourself.

Yet, I wonder if the need to know who you truly are in this lineage will ache in you as strongly as it has in me. There are still undiscovered truths about the women in our family, and some part of me believes we will feel compelled to find and face them together. Soon, my sweet baby girl, your life will start. On that day, in that very hour, with your first breath, our journey will begin. Until then, I wait for you, Alexis Lisa James, with excitement, with wonder, and, for the first time, with hope.